MAY 5, 2
For CHRIS
C
William P. Robertson

DARK HAUNTED DAY

More Tales of Terror
by

William P. Robertson

Copyright © 2006 by William P. Robertson

ISBN 978-0-7414-3234-6

Published by:

PUBLISHING.COM

Info@buybooksontheweb.com
www.buybooksontheweb.com
Toll-free (877) BUY BOOK
Local Phone (610) 941-9999
Fax (610) 941-9959

Printed in the United States of America

Published November 2012

CREDITS

The stories and poems listed below were published in the following periodicals:

"Even More Frightened," Edgar, Bloomfield, NJ;

"The Good Ship Death," Cenotaph, Leesburg, VA;

"The Elementary Librarian," evernight, North Miami Beach, FL;

"The Ratcatcher," Heart Attack, Methuen, MA;

"Trapped," Alien Skin webzine;

"The Sending," EOD, Melbourne, Australia;

"You (Poltergeist)," The Black Abyss, Philadelphia, PA;

"Edgar's Vacuum," Antithesis, Marietta, PA;

"An Empty Chair," Goddess of the Bay, Warwick, RI;

"The Eighth Wonder of the World," The Bradford Era, Bradford, PA.

Special thanks to David Rimer and Jill Bressan who helped edit these tales. This book would not have been possible without their hard work and dedication. Thanks also to Elsie Robertson for providing the history of the Lightning House.

Landscape and cover photos by William P. Robertson. Author photo by Jill Bressan. Kinzua Viaduct photographs courtesy of Dick Robertson. Photo ending "The Eighth Wonder of the World" shows my grandmother, Bernadine Johnson, on the right. Her Swedish folktales were a major inspiration for my first original horror stories.

EVEN MORE FRIGHTENED

Sleet-smeared ghosts
strangle in the slipstream.
They gurgle, gasp & groan
as they boil the sky black.
Dire is their distress.
Even more frightened are we.

CONTENTS

RESCUE AT THE DEVIL'S DEN

"If someone would stop throwing gumdrops long enough to listen," barked tour guide Pitts, staring angrily at the smirking, fat kid in the backseat of the bus, "I would like to tell you about the Valley of Death we are now entering."

"Yeah, throwin' stuff is rude, Stevie," said Gregory, elbowing the scrawny boy next to him in an effort to pass the blame. "Pay attention to the man. He knows everything about the Civil War. I'll bet he was at Fort Sumter when the first shot was fired."

Scoutmaster Morgan fixed Greg with a withering glare. Afterward, he growled, "You're not fooling anyone, Gregory Battles. I'll bet your granddad would be greatly disappointed in your behavior. Maybe I should call him when we get back to Wellsboro."

Greg glanced sheepishly at the furious scoutmaster and then muttered something behind his hand that made Stevie snicker. Only after Mr. Morgan stood and took a step toward them did the lads assume the proper decorum.

To avoid further conflict, Greg pretended to pay attention to the bearded Mr. Pitts when he gestured out the window and droned, "We are now on Crawford Avenue. To your left you will see a boulder-strewn hill called Little Round Top where some of the fiercest fighting took place here at Gettysburg. On Day Two of this epic battle, a determined group of Pennsylvania volunteers positioned on Little Round Top stopped an all-out Confederate assault meant to turn the Union's left flank. After repulsing the Rebels' charge, the troops of General Samuel Crawford counterattacked, drove the Confederates down the slope, and

1

pushed them on across the marshy valley bottom where you see Plum Run meandering along not far from this road. The fighting was grim and often involved bayonets and rifle butts when muskets misfired or couldn't be loaded fast enough. Some men's deaths were so violent and sudden that their ghosts were set loose to roam Gettysburg forever. Spectres rose everywhere about this valley running red with soldiers' blood and are still seen today by those attuned to the supernatural."

As the Scouts gawked out the windows to follow the guide's narration, Gregory pulled a thick rubber band from his pocket, stretched it out to full length, and snapped Stevie wickedly on the ear. The surprised boy's scream punctuated the historian's frightful tale of disembodied souls. His tears brought a shower of catcalls and taunts of "Do ghosts scare little Stevie?" Soon chants of "P-o-o-r Stevie! P-o-o-r Stevie!" roared from every corner of the bus.

Red-faced, the tour guide howled for silence. It took the badgering of the scoutmaster and several adult chaperones before order was restored. Afterward, Mr. Pitts cleared his throat twice and yelped, "Off to the right, you will see the Rebel stronghold known as the Devil's Den. From this rock formation, Confederate snipers shot Union officers and artillerymen over a quarter of a mile away on the summit of Little Round Top."

"Yeah right!" said Gregory while faking a cough. Then he whispered to Stevie until a ripple of laughter replaced the glum boy's sullenness.

"What's so funny?" cried Mr. Morgan, leaping into the aisle. "I swear, I'd like to throttle you, Steven Mack! What did Gregory say? Well?"

"T-T-That he could h-h-hit a Yank with his s-s-squirt g-g-gun from here, too. . ."

"Is that so, Gregory? Normally, we stop and allow our scouts to explore the snipers' positions at the Devil's Den, but your behavior has made that impossible. It's too bad your whole troop will have to miss seeing this amazing natural fort."

Again, all eyes fastened on Stevie Mack and Greg Battles. As the scouts screamed to vilify them, Mr. Morgan growled, "It looks like you boys don't want lunch either. One more outburst, and I'll see that's arranged."

In a gloomy silence, the bus wound around a sharp curve encircling a jumble of gray boulders splotched with lichen. This now forbidden landmark of the Devil's Den made every lad itch to climb the erosion-smooth rocks and worm through the crevasses. Every patch of brush and pile of boulders that could have hidden a single Rebel sharpshooter looked inviting. Stevie and Greg stared longingly out the rear window until the rock formation disappeared from view.

"Cripe, if we hadn't watched that keen battle this mornin', I'd be ready to go home," whispered the fat boy to his pal.

"Yeah, the reenactors were really great! Too bad we couldn'ta talked to them Yanks an' Rebs an' looked at their guns, an' uniforms, an' stuff. Everything they had was true to history accordin' to Mr. Pitts."

"Myself, I wish that dang Pitts was history," snickered Gregory. "Then we wouldn't have to listen to all his Little Round Top and Valley of Death crap. I already know everything he told us, anyhow."

"Sure ya do. . ."

After rolling past a display of cannon, the bus entered a dense wood. Here, it circled past several more monuments and then braked to a stop before an impressive statue of a Union soldier. The soldier struck a confident pose with his left arm held akimbo. Gripping a long musket in his right hand, he stared off into the distance as if he'd just whipped the whole Confederate army by himself.

"What's that on the statue's hat?" asked Stevie.

"Looks like a hot dog in a bun to me," chuckled Greg. "I must be hungrier than I thought."

"No, Mr. Battles," corrected Scoutmaster Morgan. "If you bothered to read the inscription, you'd see it's a buck tail. It symbolizes the shooting ability of these men, who often survived by killing deer for food before the Civil War. The regiment wearing these tails on their kepi caps came from Northwestern Pennsylvania and are a proud part of our state's heritage. That's why we stopped here to show you this monument. I myself had a Bucktail relative who was wounded here at Gettysburg."

"Yeah, the Bucktails were excellent marksmen," agreed the tour guide. "They usually served as skirmishers for the Union Army."

"What's that mean?" asked Stevie.

"It means they were scouts who went out looking for the Rebels and often encountered the enemy first. They were like today's elite Army Rangers."

"The Bucktails must have been real tough then, huh?"

"That's right, Mr. Mack," replied the scoutmaster. "Why, at Harrisonburg they ran smack dab into an entire Confederate brigade. Although outnumbered five-to-one, they killed General Turner Ashby and five hundred of his soldiers. It wasn't until half the Bucktails lay wounded on the ground that they were forced to retreat."

"Wow!"

"And at Antietam," continued Mr. Morgan, "they engaged the Rebels the evening before the main battle began. After being raked by wicked cannon fire, they chased the Southerners into the East Wood and had to lay there all night to hold the enemy at bay. The Bucktails distinguished themselves even further at Fredericksburg. While the rest of the Union army got whipped soundly by Robert E. Lee, the First Pennsylvania Rifles were the only Yankee troops to break through the Confederate lines stretched out on the high ground above the Rappahannock River."

"Who were the First Pennsylvania Rifles?" asked a wide-eyed lad, tugging at the scoutmaster's elbow.

"I'm sorry. I didn't mean to confuse you. That's another name the Bucktails went by, along with the Thirteenth Pennsylvania Reserves."

"But by the time they fought at Gettysburg, they had joined the Federal Army," reminded Mr. Pitts. "They were then known as the 42nd Pennsylvania."

"Did the Bucktails fight the Rebs first in this battle, too?" asked Stevie.

"No, they were stationed near Washington when Lee's army began his invasion of the North, so they had a long, hot march to get here. After a week's trek, the Bucktails still had to hike all night to arrive in time to join the battle on Day Two. Can you imagine marching ten miles in wool uniforms, lugging heavy rifles, blankets and haversacks, and then fighting a battle? And they didn't have much time to sleep, either!"

"Can't we eat now?" grumbled Gregory. "The only

5

battle I wanna win is with my growlin' stomach."

"Aw-w-w! Let's hear why they built this monument for the Bucktails first," pleaded Stevie, remembering the smack Battles had given him on his ear. "You can wait a little longer, can't ya, Greg?"

"I'm glad that you're interested," smiled the guide. "The 42nd Pennsylvania definitely deserved to be recognized for its role here. The regiment held the extreme left flank of the Union line on Little Round Top and helped drive the Rebels from the summit back across the Valley of Death to the Devil's Den. It might have even chased the Rebs from there if darkness hadn't fallen. The regiment's colonel at one point was well in advance of the other charging Yanks, leading by his brave example--"

"Thank you, Mr. Pitts," interrupted the scoutmaster. "I hate to stop your fascinating tale, but I think we better have lunch before our own troops get too restless. This is as good a place as any for us to stretch our legs, too."

With an exuberant shout, the scouts leaped from their seats and pushed up the aisle, nearly trampling Mr. Morgan and the bearded historian in their stampede. The boys charged off the bus and romped about the Bucktail statue while the adults unloaded cardboard boxes stuffed with sandwiches, apples, bananas, cookies, and grapes. When the lads surged forward to be fed, a displeased chaperone observed wryly, "You'd think it was our boys who had marched all night to get to Gettysburg. They act like they haven't eaten since leaving Wellsboro yesterday morning."

"The way they're pushing, I'll bet they'd settle for the slimy salt pork and weevily hardtack the Civil War soldiers ate," grunted Mr. Pitts.

"I'm just glad we're serving lemonade instead of Coca-Cola," replied Morgan, "or they'd want to reenact Pickett's Charge."

Just then, Gregory crowded up to the scoutmaster to get his lunch. "I'm sorry for throwin' stuff on the bus, sir," he mumbled. "I must have left my manners at home."

"Apology accepted, Mr. Battles. Now, move along.

We have a schedule to keep."

Stevie Mack squirmed from the jostling mob next. His box lunch barely touched his hand when Gregory began herding him toward a small marker to the left of the Bucktail monument where no one else sat. The marker resembled a tombstone. It had a Bucktail cap and an epitaph carved on in. Greg scanned the inscription and then whispered to the boy he had corralled, "While the grownups are busy, why don't we sneak off to the Devil's Den and eat?"

"But w-w-what if we get caught?" stammered Stevie Mack.

"We'll never be missed if just the two of us go. Come on. It's not that far."

"I-I-I don't know. . ."

"Hey, you wanna see where the snipers hid out, don't ya?"

"I guess. . ."

"Then let's go!"

"Are you sure we won't get in trouble?"

"Come on, you sissy! Nobody'll notice."

"But I don't wanna go where all those d-d-dead guys were."

"Then you better not sit here either," said Gregory, "because a Bucktail officer bit the dust on this very spot."

Stevie leaped from the marker he'd had his back against, and Battles led him along the fringe of the crowd that nearly engulfed the bus. Next, the two boys nonchalantly wandered off down the road, using the mob to shield their progress from the swamped adults. They pretended to be interested in a neighboring monument erected from three huge boulders for the 5th New Hampshire Regiment. When no one yelled after them, they disappeared behind the monument and lit out for the Devil's Den.

The boys kept to the brush until they could no longer hear the impatient voices of the boisterous scouts. Returning to the road, they walked briskly along munching on sandwiches between triumphant snorts of laughter. While they finished their lunches, Greg stopped to inspect a display of field cannon and a monument featuring a Union artilleryman holding a ramrod.

"Come on!" urged Stevie nervously. "Let's get goin'! It looks like it's gonna rain."

"Keep your shirt on," grunted the fat boy. "My granddad used to be a battlefield guide here until he had heart trouble. He taught me all about Civil War cannons an' stuff. He knows way more than old Pitts. I wanna have a good look at these Parrots. Or are they three inch ordnance guns? Let me see. . ."

Stevie Mack continued to badger his friend while Greg inspected the field pieces. Ignoring Stevie's pleas, Greg pretended to load one. It wasn't until Battles pulled an imaginary lanyard and fired his cannon that he finally took to his heels. Despite his size, the boy could really run, and Stevie had a hard time keeping up. He chugged along behind the heavy lad until they bolted around a corner and spied the jumble of rocks they'd seen from the bus window.

"Wow! Them boulders are really high," gasped Stevie, staring at the rocks towering above him. "An' look at how many hidin' places there are here. There's even walls made outta stones. No wonder they call this place the Devil's Den."

"A sniper hid behind those walls," explained Gregory. "He called them his 'home.' An' look! There's pit marks made by return fire. Ya know what kind of guns the Rebs used to shoot Yankees on Little Round Top, don't ya?"

"No."

"Target rifles that weighed over thirty pounds."

"Like your gut, ya mean?" razzed Stevie with a nervous laugh.

"An' they had long octagon barrels an' twenty power scopes. That's why those guns were so accurate."

"How do you know? You're just pullin' my leg, aren't ya?"

"No, I swear it's the truth. My granddad told me all about target rifles, too. I'm not really dumb. I just pretend to be. . .sometimes. Can you imagine how the kids would pick on me if I was fat <u>and</u> a smarty-pants?"

8

"We still have to visit a museum this afternoon. I'll bet we'll see a target rifle there. Maybe we outta get back now before we get left behind. An' look at that sky. It's gettin' b-b-blacker by the minute."

"No! No! Let's climb to the top of those rocks before we go an' get a real view of Little Round Top. We could pretend we're snipers and pop a few Yanks."

"I wouldn't wanna do that. After hearin' what Mr. Morgan said about the Bucktails, I'd rather be one of them than a dang Reb. Let's go back. Please!"

"Hey, I came here to climb these rocks, and that's what I'm gonna do!"

"But what if we fall?"

"We're not gonna fall. Are you a baby, or what?"

With a haughty shake of his head, Gregory started up a gentle incline that led to the top of the first set of boulders. When Stevie saw how easy the path was to climb, he clambered behind his friend and reached the summit without breaking a sweat.

"Wow! That sure was a long way them snipers had to shoot," croaked the smaller boy, staring at the rocky hill across the valley. "I think our guide said it was a quarter mile."

"That's why I'll bet the braver Rebs went out on the next point," said Battles, gesturing toward the rock ahead.

"But they'd have to jump across that c-c-crevice to get there. It has to be f-f-five-feet wide!"

"Ahhh! Anyone can make it if he doesn't look down. You know, I wonder why I hang out with you. All you do is whine like a girl. I think I'll start callin' you Stevena."

"Who are you callin' a girl? I can run an' jump better than most guys in my gym class. Coach Green even says so."

"Well, go ahead. Prove it!" badgered Battles. "Jump over to that other point. It's flat as the top of a table. Even Stevena can't get hurt landing there."

"Okay, I will!"

Stevie measured the jump across the wide crevice with his eyes. After brushing away some loose gravel that littered the ledge, he backed up to get a running start. With a determined cry, he shot forward and leaped with all his might toward the flat point ahead. He flew across the deep fissure and landed on his feet well beyond it. He put on the brakes and stumbled several feet farther before coming to a halt inches from the cliff at the end of the rock formation. Afterward, he spun around and stammered, "I-I-I did it, Greg. Now, it's your turn."

"Not before you leap back over here again," replied Battles with a weak smile.

"Back over again?"

"Yeah, it's not smart for both of us to get trapped out there."

"Trapped?"

"I was just teasin'," confessed Gregory. "I didn't think you'd really jump."

Looking toward his friend, Stevie saw that the rock he was on was much lower than the one he had jumped from. In order to return to safety, he had to leap over the crevice and up to a two-foot higher ledge. His mouth flew open at the discovery, and his legs turned to water. With a deep groan, he melted to his knees and cried, "How am I gonna get offa here? How? How?"

"Don't ask me," replied Gregory, helplessly kneading his hands. "Maybe I oughta get help."

"Hey, don't l-l-leave me!"

"But it's startin' to rain. You'll never get off those rocks once they get slippery."

"Slippery?"

"You heard me. I gotta go."

Before Mack could further persuade him, a rumble of thunder sent Battles scurrying for the path that led to safety down the back of the Devil's Den. He had no sooner disappeared from Stevie's view when a heavy downpour began to pound against the rocks. It was followed by flashes of lightning from across the Valley of Death. Remembering a page from the scout handbook, Stevie immediately flopped on his belly and flattened himself out on the rock.

The boy burst into tears as the cold rain pummeled

him, and a gusting wind whipped his drenched clothes. Shivering uncontrollably, he blubbered, "I gotta get off this point. I just gotta!"

Stevie continued to sob until he saw a tall figure emerge on top of the ledge recently vacated by Battles. The man was dressed in a stained, tattered uniform of Yankee blue. He had a youthful face and kind, hazel eyes. His dark hair and goatee made his fair skin look even more pallid. Despite his youth, the soldier carried himself with an air of authority that caused Stevie to notice the colonel's eagles sewn on the shoulders of his uniform.

"It looks like you got yourself into a pickle, laddie," shouted the young officer. "Don't worry. I'm here to help."

"You a Bucktail reenactor?" cried the boy, seeing the white tail sewn on the colonel's kepi cap.

"Yes, I'm a Bucktail. Fred Taylor to be exact."

"I'm S-S-Stevie Mack. Everybody's gonna call me 'Stupid' when they f-f-find me."

"Don't run yourself into the ground, laddie. You jumped out there on a dare, didn't you?"

"Yes, sir. How do you know?"

"I did plenty of foolish things myself for the same reason. I couldn't seem to help it. I was impetuous by nature. Like the time I gave myself up to the Rebs at Harrisonburg to tend the wounds of Colonel Kane. I was just a captain then and took some real kidding from the Bucktails after I got exchanged."

"Wow! You take your reenactin' seriously. I watched your battle this mornin', and, boy, did it look real with the cannons blastin' an' smoke rollin' an' bayonets shinin' in the sun. All that hand-to-hand fightin' looked real, too. You must be really brave."

"And I'll bet you're a brave lad, too, Stevie. You're related to Samuel Mack, aren't you?"

"How do you know I had a great uncle Sammy?"

"I knew him back in '61, and you're his spittin' image when he was a might younger."

"And you say he was brave?" asked Stevie as the rain

11

stopped, and the sun burst through the clouds like a glowing ball of fire.

"Didn't you know he fought at Gettysburg? After we chased the Rebs into the woods over yonder, it was your uncle who went forward to scout out their position just before it got dark. After all the fighting he'd been through that day, he wanted to make sure the enemy didn't outflank the rest of us Bucktails and cut us to pieces."

"You say I look like him?"

"Yes, an uncanny likeness. Now, let's get you back to safety."

"A-A-Are you sure you're up to it?" stuttered Stevie, noticing the deep crimson stain on the breast of the other's coat. "Did you hurt yourself in t-t-today's reenactment?"

"Just a scratch, laddie."

"Okay. I guess I'm r-r-ready if you are."

"Then get up and walk to the far end of that point. It shouldn't be slippery now," said the colonel, pointing to the steam of evaporating moisture rising from the rocks in the sunshine.

Stevie wobbled to his feet and took one fearful step. When his canvas sneakers didn't slide, he took another and another until his confidence returned. With a weak grin, he walked as far as he dared toward the end of the point. After what seemed like an eternity, he turned to face the colonel, who continued to shout encouragement.

"Alright, Private Mack. When I give the command, run as fast as your legs will carry you. Remember. Jump high. Go!"

Stevie tore off across the top of the rock. He rushed through the rising steam until he was at the very brink of the wide crevice separating him from the beckoning officer. Then he launched himself into the air and flew toward the other ledge. He hit the opposite rock with a terrific thud that knocked the air from his lungs. His toes churned in the loose gravel, and he clawed for a handhold on anything that would keep him from pitching backward into the yawning fissure he had cleared by only a couple inches. He felt himself sliding backward into the abyss when a pale hand shot out and dragged him to safety.

For many minutes Stevie Mack lay shivering in his own sweat. Pain throbbed from his skinned knees and elbows, and his heart pounded from his close call. When he finally looked up to thank his rescuer, he found himself alone on the rocks.

Still trembling, the lad staggered to his feet and peered down the backside of the Devil's Den. Below him, he saw the tall colonel striding toward the path that led to the Bucktail Monument. Before Stevie could yell to him, the soldier vanished into the thick woods.

Blinking back tears, the boy tottered down the incline leading from the jumble of rocks. He hadn't gone far before he heard voices rushing toward him. The next minute he found himself being mobbed by Gregory Battles, Mr. Morgan, and a dozen scouts.

"So ya saved yourself, did ya?" shouted Greg, slapping his friend wildly on the shoulder. "Ya saved yourself! Saved yourself!"

"I'm so glad you're okay!" cried the scoutmaster, with a relieved grin. "Why, you're soaking wet. That rain sure came down. Here! Throw this blanket around your shoulders before you catch your death of cold."

"D-D-Did any of you see a Bucktail soldier?" asked Stevie, through chattering teeth. "H-H-He was headed right toward you."

"We didn't see anyone," said Battles.

"But ya musta passed him," insisted the lad. "I saw him come this way."

"Passed who?" asked Mr. Morgan, handing Stevie a thermos of lemonade.

"Colonel Taylor is who. He's the one who saved me."

"Colonel Fred Taylor?" cried Gregory, his fat face turning suddenly white. "That can't be!"

"What do ya mean it c-c-can't?"

"We sat at <u>his</u> memorial before we sneaked off. Taylor was killed here in the woods on July 2, 1863. . ."

13

THE GREAT STAG

The lone hunter slid noiselessly from a thicket of scrub beech and entered a path that wound up a steep mountain choked with brush and trees. The man was clad in a raveled blanket coat and a pair of stained wool pants. A knit cap was crammed over an unruly mop of bootblack hair. A smile played across his weather-cracked lips as he admired the fresh snowfall that made the day perfect for tracking and hunting. After adjusting the scoped rifle cradled in his left arm, he again set his gum boots in motion.

The half-breed worked methodically up the mountain. Often, he stopped to scan the woods around him for the elusive deer he stalked. Each time he paused, he put his back against a trailside tree trunk to conceal his outline. Soon, he began to encounter fresh hoof prints that spilled from the mountainside across his path. That made him even more alert and slowed his pace to a veritable crawl.

The hunter inched his way along until spotting a distinctively wide set of boot prints that entered the trail from a bisecting road. Glancing warily from left to right, he felt a sudden sweat pop out on his forehead. Before he could bolt for the nearest brush, a warden clad in dark green camo stepped out from behind a broad oak to block his escape.

"Where ya goin', Blackie Grimes?" demanded the officer, his hand straying toward the pistol housed on his hip.

"Uh. . .Feeggered I'd follow theze deer, Luke," muttered the half-breed, pointing toward a set of pronounced tracks veering up the slope.

"Yeah, right! Where's yer orange clothin'? After I give ya a warnin' an' a fine, ya know durn well that it's illegal ta hunt without it."

"Right here, meester," grunted Grimes, turning to reveal a patch of faded blaze cloth stitched crudely to the back of his coat. "I'm wearin' two hundred feefty square eenches of orange. . .like the rule book says. You can measure eff you want."

"That don't cut it! You know as well as me that the orange must be visible from all di-rections. Looks like I get ta run ya in."

"But I's way leegal," protested Blackie. "Lookee here."

The half-breed bowed toward Warden Luke. Atop his knit cap was pinned a scrap of reddish yellow yarn that technically fulfilled the limits of the law.

Grumbling to himself, the officer said, "The only difference 'tween you an' a coyote is that you smell worse. But you'll screw up. An' I know you already done potted two deer."

"Even coyotes must eat!" snapped Blackie, forgetting the <u>five</u> bucks and the doe he had already shot. Fire blazed in his sullen eyes at the insult. He glared at the tall warden and tightened his grip on his gunstock.

"Yeah, but at least them predators know who's the big dog," growled the lawman, drawing himself up to his full height. "What are ya doin' in these here woods anyhow if'n ya already got them two deer I knowed you shot?"

"Why, I has ze bonus tag," replied the half-breed, again turning to show Luke the extra license holder pinned on his back.

"Which en-titles ya to one extra doe. I'll be watching ya, Grimes. You best believe it!"

"Then you best be able to drive ze truck to the top of that mountain," chuckled Grimes, motioning toward Luke's pickup that was half concealed by a patch of beech farther down the bisecting road. "That's where I do ze good hunting."

"Ya don't think I can hike up there?" snarled the lanky officer. "Why, I can still walk the legs off a little runt

16

like you any day o' the week, includin' Sunday. See ya at the top. You bet!"

"See you in ze fires of hell!" yipped Blackie, giving the warden a mock salute and a thumb to the nose.

Before the lawman could bark back, Grimes leaped into the nearest thicket and bolted straight up a severe incline that most bears couldn't have climbed. Using saplings and branches for handholds, he struggled upward until he reached the next bench. There, he collapsed in the snow, listening to Luke's faint, windblown curses below.

When the half-breed's breathing returned to normal, he staggered to his feet and found another faint trail that wound around the mountain. Again, he assumed a hunter's stealth and crept along searching the woods with his piercing, pitch-colored eyes. He continued on until he reached the next trail that led steeply upward to the summit. There were deer tracks everywhere, and he licked his cracked lips knowing that he soon would be among the fat doe that swarmed on the ridge top.

Blackie's heart thudded with excitement when he spied a rusted oil tank capsized in the snow ahead. Just behind the overturned tank sat an abandoned powerhouse that marked the beginning of the best hunting territory. The building was made of tin, and its door yawned open to reveal a long-silent engine that once powered ten creaking rod lines and oil jacks. Now, the powerhouse provided winter refuge for skunks and other small critters. The half-breed grinned as he watched a startled squirrel dart inside. Then he stomped toward the beech thicket that crowned the peak beyond.

Keeping to the trail, Grimes slunk through a sea of rattling, orange leaves. He moved a step at a time, keeping his eyes trained on the path ahead. He hadn't gone more than a quarter mile when he saw a doe's nose poke from the brush only fifty yards distant. To avoid detection, the hunter slipped into the prone position. He stared through the scope and snicked his rifle off safe.

The lead doe crept stiffly from the beech, sniffing the

air for enemies. Cautiously, she peered in all directions before moving to the middle of the trail. Behind her were two yearlings that followed rotely in trusting obedience. The herd barely stepped into the open when the roar of Blackie's .30-40 Krag rent the silence with deadly thunder.

The doe's head exploded in a cloud of hair and gore, and she crashed unmoving to the ground. With stunned bleats, her young ones milled about, staring stupidly into the brush ahead with wild, panicked eyes. As they sidled side-by-side toward their downed mother, a second shot rang out. It was the last sound either of them was to hear. The bullet tore through the neck of the first yearling and then entered the second just above the front shoulder. Both small doe collapsed in a spray of blood to kick weakly and gurgle one last astonished cry.

Blackie was up and racing toward the deer the instant they fell from the cross hairs of his scope. "Show me a coyote that could do that," cackled the half-breed, still fuming over the warden's insult. "I kill with ze efficiency no beast can match!"

Grimes whipped out a long, wicked-looking skinning knife. He slit each deer's throat in turn to make sure all were good and dead. "Now, I got meat--'til strawberries make ze venison sweet again," he whispered, glancing warily down the trail toward the powerhouse. "Must hide theze. Queek! Luke must not see."

The half-breed dragged the mother doe over to a great gray beech blown down by a recent squall. He dug furiously in the snow beneath the trunk and then crammed the deer's carcass in the space he had created. Similarly, he concealed the body of one of the yearlings beneath a neighboring windfall. When he returned to the road to fetch the second small doe, a flight of chickadees sailed from the brush and began circling Blackie's head. The birds beat their wings furiously, calling with angry "deedeedees." They closed within inches of the man's face, slapping at him with their feathers. Their attack was so fierce and persistent that Grimes was forced to drop his gun into the snow to cover his head with both arms. Again and again the chickadees dove at him until finally he lashed out with a big, mittened paw and knocked one of his antagonists from mid-flight.

"What ze hell is wrong with you?" howled the half-breed, stomping the chickadee beneath his gum boots. "Since when such happy birds go crazy?"

The other birds continued to dive at Grimes, who danced and slapped like a honey bear beset by bees. They did not let up their assault until one-by-one they were batted from the sky and tramped into bloody pulps.

Fuming and covered with sweat, Blackie hid the second yearling with her sister. Still distracted, he broke off a branch and brushed away his tracks that led to his deer caches. After wiping out signs of the does' demise from the snowy road, he stooped to pick up his rifle where the chickadees had attacked him. Cursing in both English and Iroquois, he knocked the snow from the barrel. Next, he cleaned the lens of his scope with a soiled, blue handkerchief that he yanked roughly from his pants pocket. When the .30-40 Krag was safe to fire again, he grunted, "Too early to quit ze hunt. Still have bonus tag. Ha! Ha!"

Blackie cast several furtive glances down the trail behind him. Afterward, he prowled along the ridge looking for more venison on the hoof. His eyes had a murderous cast as he slipped noiselessly through the powdery snow. He skulked along, stopping often to survey the winter-quiet woods. Finally, he paused by a patch of bloodred brambles to blow his nose. As he fished for the oft-used handkerchief, a scolding male grouse erupted from the thicket inches from where Grimes stood. With a surprised gasp, the half-breed leaped back, lost his footing, and toppled to the frozen ground, cracking his skull on a rock. A darkness descended from above and below as the rush of wings dissipated down a black slope.

After what seemed like a very long time, Grime's eyes fluttered open. His vision blurred at each attempt to raise his head, and he was forced to sink groaning back into the snow. It took him six tries before he could sit up. When he finally fought to his feet a half-hour later, he shook his fist in the direction the grouse had flown. "Doddamn you!" he growled. "I come back. You wait! With my shotgun I git you. Warden not always on patrol."

Grimes knocked the snow from his rifle a second time and lurched woozily forward. He hadn't taken more than a step or two when a pileated woodpecker gave a loud, warning cry. The alarm was immediately taken up by a red squirrel and then by blue jays as the half-breed slogged up the ridge. With so many creatures announcing his presence, Grimes stomped angrily through the snow. Finally, he broke into a wolf's lope to lose the pesky sentinels. He trotted and then sprinted with the sharp, reproving voices dogging him. On and on he rumbled, losing track of time and consciousness. The cries seemed to grow louder, the faster he ran.

Grimes raced up the trail until blackness crowded his vision. With a spent grunt, he fell on his face and lay motionless until a swirling wind revived him. When he crawled groggily to all fours, he found himself in a part of the forest he had never hunted. Here, the deadfalls lay buried beneath heavy caskets of snow. Rotted, hollow-trunked beeches leered at him with knot hole faces, and grave groves of hemlocks creaked in the stiff breeze. A pounding headache magnified this creaking until Blackie put his hands over his ears to shut out the grating sound.

A stiff wind probed Grime's blanket coat like icy corpse fingers. To escape its chilling velocity, he staggered to his feet and followed an oft-used deer trail into a thickly wooded hollow below the ridge top. There, he discovered fresh deer sign everywhere. Tracks crisscrossed the forest floor and led to widespread diggings made by hungry buck and doe. With acorns as thick as marbles beneath the disturbed snow, it was no secret to Blackie why so many deer congregated in such a small yard. He took a second to examine the lofty oaks that towered over him and then returned to his cruel business. Ignoring the pounding in his temples, he looked for a good point of ambush on a prominent crossing.

The half-breed had barely concealed himself behind a massive hemlock when a faint wailing reached his ears. He strained to listen until the cries of "Help! Help!" echoed from the ridge behind him. As the voices drew nearer, they assumed the high-pitched key of lost children. Finally, the carousel of haunted wails swirled directly overhead. With the sky alive with anguish, Blackie felt the gooseflesh rise on his extremities, and he hunkered closer to the trunk that sheltered him.

Doubting his own sanity, Grimes glanced upward and saw the boiling clouds part to reveal a broken flight of geese flailing the dark sky with their wings. Grinning uneasily, he snapped his rifle off safe and muttered, "So it's you who cause ze racket. Must be echo of hollow that makes you sound like leetle kids. I should knock you from ze flight for scaring Blackie so!"

Although spooked, Grimes shifted his scrutiny to the deer crossing he hoped would bring him a huge buck. He had seen fresh scrapings on every sapling he had passed since entering this mountain sag. By the length and breadth of these buck rubs, he knew they had been made by more than a spike or four point polishing its antlers. He licked his lips greedily at the thought of such a buck and tried to control the shaking that still made aiming his rifle a chore.

Grimes raised his .30-40 Krag and peered through the scope. Carefully, he looked down the trail to make sure he had a clear shooting lane. No sentinel birds gave him away this time as a foreboding silence gripped the entire wood. It wasn't long before he discerned the faint crunching of snow just below him to his left. With his pulse pounding in his ears, he raised his rifle again only to find the scope completely fogged. As he dug frantically for his handkerchief, the heavy footsteps of the approaching beast grew louder and louder and LOUDER.

Just as the head of a Great Stag popped over the rise, Blackie yanked his hankerchief free and began swabbing madly at his obscured lens. Not that he needed any magnification to see the massive rack bobbing toward him atop the hugest deer he had encountered in twenty years of hunting. The buck's back was a good five feet high, and its legs were big around as a draft horse's. Enraged grunts rose from the beast's brawny, white throat. Steam poured from its flared nostrils. Its eyes had a mad cast to them. The antlers appeared even more impressive with each powerful step the buck took. Blackie's mouth flew open in amazement when he counted twenty-five points on the wicked-looking horns.

No matter how hard the half-breed rubbed his scope lens, he could not rid it of fog. The stag now closed within fifty feet and dropped its head to charge the quivering hunter. With the pounding of hooves throbbing in Blackie's skull, he whipped up his rifle and blindly yanked the trigger. Instead of the roar he expected, there was the sick thud of a firing pin striking a dud cartridge.

Before Grimes could chamber another round, the huge buck rose on its hind legs and lashed out with its left, front hoof. The blow smashed Blackie's nose to jam and shook the rifle from his quivering hands. As the hunter tottered, spewing blood, a swirling wind filled the hollow with a strange, priest-like chant. "I am Divine," it droned. "I am Divine."

The buck punched with its other front hoof, knocking out Grime's teeth. As more gore squirted from his pulverized face, the half-breed suddenly remembered the three does he had slaughtered on the ridge. With a whimper, he dropped to his knees and raised his hands in a prayerful, pleading pose.

The Great Stag bent down and thrust its saber-like antlers through Blackie's chest. The next instant Grimes was lifted flailing into the air. He gurgled as blood filled his lungs. Flung skyward like a broken scarecrow, he emitted a hollow, helpless shriek. He hit the ground heavily, staring wide-eyed at the snorting, outraged beast towering above him. Then there was nothing but blackness as a flurry of hooves hammered him into the gory snow.

22

About an hour later, a warden dressed in green camouflage slipped to the lip of the hollow. Luke had been following Blackie's footprints for miles, and he paused to catch his breath and listen to the creaking of the frozen trees.

"Ain't never knowed an Indian ta hunt in a place like this," whispered the warden, noting the knothole faces glowering from a stand of rotted beech. "Grimes must be addled by the fall I saw he took back yonder. . .or outta his stinkin' mind!"

To calm his apprehension, the lanky warden concentrated on following the half-breed's boot tracks. They led him down a well-pronounced deer trail into the bowels of a dank oak grove interspersed with witch-haired hemlocks. There, the tracks were more difficult to follow, often disappearing among a multitude of fresh deer diggings.

As Luke glanced about the spooky glen, a grim smile flickered on his face. He grinned again when he remembered the strange way he had found the does cached by the half-breed just beyond the powerhouse. He still could not believe that in the middle of the day a nocturnal owl had swooped and knocked off his hat, forcing him to stop where a faint spray of deer blood stained the trail. Then some nuthatches squawked and carried on so in the underbrush that the officer went there to investigate. Just a single drop of gore near a half-swept boot track led to his discovery of the two yearlings. With that, the warden had enough evidence to lift Blackie's hunting license and keep him out of the woods for a very long time.

"Serve the bugger right!" muttered Luke with a renewed burst of energy. "I'm gonna love bustin' Grimes' be-hind once I catches up with 'im."

The lawman sneaked a little faster, taking long, silent strides through the snow. It had become eerily quiet, and he swore he heard the excited "deedeedees" of a ghostly flock of chickadees as he slipped along. Although he peered intently into the oak branches above him, he caught not one glimpse of the black-capped birds.

Finally, the warden rounded a bend and found where

Grime's boot tracks came to an abrupt halt. At the exact moment he spotted the horribly mauled body of the half-breed, a blast of icy wind stabbed through his coat. With chattering teeth, Luke bent to examine what was left of the poacher he had hunted for so long. Blackie's entire face was bashed in. His front teeth were missing. His nose was mashed gristle. One eye socket was vacant. The other housed an inky pupil bulged in unspeakable agony.

Luke turned and vomited into the snow. Wiping his mouth on his mitten, he continued his examination. It was then that he saw the jagged wound ripped by huge antlers the length of Blackie's chest.

"So a buck got 'im, eh?" grunted Luke. "An' here I figgered some ticked off landowner beat him to a pulp. The little bugger musta poured a whole bottle of doe scent on himself to get a buck so riled. Yet, I don't smell nothin'. . ."

The officer ran his hands over Grimes' rent ribs and on down his legs. Every major bone in his body had been shattered by what Luke concluded were wicked hoof blows. When the grunts of a great buck resounded up the gully below him, he snatched a stout rope from his jacket pocket and tied a loop in one end. Feverishly, he worked the loop over the corpse's head, around its shoulders, and up under its armpits. Pulling the slipknot tight, he began dragging what was left of Blackie Grimes from the haunted hollow.

"No need ta get a party of fellas with a stretcher," muttered Luke, glancing nervously about. "Ain't e-nough left of Grimes fer that. Couldn't git no durned volunteers to come here, anyhow. . ."

Luke pulled for all he was worth as the wind kicked up to wash away his last words. Its swirling intensified until it assumed the howling pitch of a living thing. "I am Divine," the wind shrieked just as Luke saw a Great Stag step from behind a hundred year old oak to shake a huge set of horns stained with bright gore.

The warden didn't remember much after that. He lowered his head and charged uphill, his legs pumping like pistons. The exact moment the rope broke, he didn't know.

Nor did he care what became of the corpse of Blackie Grimes. He had felt the breath of that Stag on the back of his neck and the breeze from those slashing antlers. All he knew is that he made it to the ridge top. Yes, and now Luke could just see the old powerhouse ahead through a rattling screen of orange beech. He still didn't dare turn around. All he could do was run. Run for the road at the foot of this very scary mountain. The mountain that killed those who violated its laws and creatures.

THE LIGHTNING HOUSE

"Ah-h-h, Pa, do we gotta live in the Lightnin' House?" grumbled Leo as his father pulled into the driveway of an ominous, two-story dwelling hugging the Pennsylvania state line. "Heck! Every kid in the Tuna Valley knows this place is haunted."

"Boo Boo, don't scare your sister with such nonsense," chastised Art Miles, seeing little Elsie's dark eyes bulge with fear.

"Yes, this is the only home we could afford to rent," reminded Mrs. Miles. "Now, be quiet!"

"And the landlord even offered to take some money off the rent if I help fix up the property," beamed the father. "He'll provide the materials if I provide the sweat. It's a good thing I'm handy with a hammer and paint brush by the look of things."

The Miles' dented Ford spun to the top of the muddy drive and stopped in front of a dilapidated dwelling half overgrown with vines. The paint on the house was badly peeled, and the back wall was blackened by a recent fire. Buckled glass in the windows refracted their image as the family crept from the auto and crossed the side yard with trepidation.

Pa Miles inserted his key in the lock, and the side door swung open with a grating creak. The scent of charred wood wormed up his nostrils, and he sneezed violently, causing his daughter to jump back from the entranceway. "We'll have to air this place out pronto, Bertha," he coughed to his wife. "You'd think the other folks who lived here could have done that. The landlord said they just moved out last week."

"Art, don't get your dander up," replied Mrs. Miles, poking her nose in the door to inspect the spacious living room and kitchen. "At least this place has plenty of room for family activities and games. A good cleaning will do wonders. You'll see."

"We ain't gonna be doin' much fun stuff if we're burnt to a crisp," groaned Leo. "Are we, Elsie?"

With a terrified look, Elsie ran and climbed her father like a tree. When safe in his arms, she sobbed, "Daddy will save me. . .if that bad ghost burns the house. Won't you, Daddy?"

"Shame on you, Boo Boo, for scaring your sister like that!" exclaimed Pa Miles. "Any house can be struck by lightning. That doesn't mean it's haunted."

"Even if this rattrap caught fire five times? I thought lightnin' never struck twice in the same place."

"Now, listen! Ghosts can't strike matches or call down lightning bolts from the sky. And, furthermore, there are no such things as ghosts. Case closed!"

"Your father is right," seconded Bertha. "Let's go upstairs and pick out our bedrooms. Even you will think that's fun, Boo Boo."

"Okay, Ma. If you say so. . ."

Mrs. Miles plucked Elsie from her father's embrace and led her by the hand past the bathroom and up a staircase leading to the second floor. The stairwell was narrow and reeked of charred wood. Leo, tagging along behind, made the passageway vibrate forebodingly with his heavy footsteps. He continued his Frankenstein stomp until tears flowed down his sister's paling cheeks. Finally, his mother snapped, "That's enough of that devilment, young man!"

The Miles emerged into a long, dank hall. As they proceeded up the cracked linoleum, they saw two doorways yawning on each side of them. Peeking into the first room on the right, the mother smiled encouragingly to her daughter and said, "This is a perfect place for my sewing machine. That big bay window will let in lots of sunshine.

27

Your father and I will sleep in the master bedroom I see across the way."

"That's where I wanna sleep, too," sobbed Elsie, digging her knuckles into her streaming eyes.

"Oh, no, dear. You need your own space for your toys and things. I'll bet the room next to ours will be perfect for you."

"Yeah, perfect for the ghost, too," joshed Leo. "He's been lookin' for a roomie ever since the last people lit out. He'll love that canopy bed of yours. He can pee in the can you keep under it and won't have to go downstairs in the dark to the bathroom."

"That will be enough of that, Boo Boo. Now, let's go help your father unpack the car."

The Miles worked all day Sunday moving into the grim, old home. It took three trips back and forth from Bradford to fetch the rest of their personal belongings. Their cousin Milton, meanwhile, brought two truckloads of furniture. By the time everything was lugged into the house and put in its proper place, the family was too exhausted to do anything but collapse in bed.

The alarm clock blasted for ten minutes before Mrs. Miles rose the next morning to fix breakfast. Another ten minutes passed before her husband straggled into the kitchen still fussing with his necktie. Leo charged downstairs moments later rattling the dishes with his pounding footsteps. Close on his heels came Elsie with her face etched with anger.

"What's eating my little girl this morning?" laughed Mr. Miles, noting his daughter's cross look. "I thought you were looking forward to the first day of school. I'll bet you'll get all A's just like last year. We're so proud of you, darling. If only your brother did half as well."

"He's who I'm mad at."

"Me?" replied Leo innocently. "What did I do?"

"Pulled off my covers, is what."

"Your covers?"

"Yeah, every time I pulled them up, you ripped them

back off me. It went on all night!"

"All night? The only thing I did all night was snore. I ain't never worked as hard as I did yesterday. I was way too tuckered out to pull no pranks."

"<u>Any</u> pranks," corrected the boy's mother.

"Okay, <u>any</u> pranks!"

"I believe you, son, despite your bad grammar. Several times I woke up to listen to the sounds of our new house and heard you sawing logs like there was no tomorrow."

"Elsie, you must have kicked off your own covers," suggested Mr. Miles. "Anyone can get restless when overtired."

"Do you believe that sneak over me?" bawled the girl, pointing to her smirking brother. "Even after the tricks he pulled last year at school?"

"I'm always gettin' blamed for stuff," sighed Leo with a martyred look.

"You mean you didn't squirt glue in the teacher's grade book or slam her hand in the boys' room door?"

"Them were accidents. . .That's why they call me Boo Boo."

"<u>Those</u> were accidents," declared Mrs. Miles. "Now, let's eat before we all start the day off on the wrong foot."

As soon as her family had rushed out the door for work and school, Bertha cleared the table and washed the breakfast dishes. Afterward, she grabbed some rags, her mop, and a bucket of soapy water and bolted upstairs to clean. She started in her son's room, which she knew would be a mess. She spent a whole hour making his bed and picking up the packing boxes he had strewn everywhere. Then it took Mrs. Miles another hour to mop up the muddy footprints Leo had tracked upstairs while moving in his things.

"I don't know what I'm going to do with that boy," muttered Bertha as she finished mopping. "After what my princess said at breakfast, I'll bet her room will look like a hurricane hit it, too."

Bertha gasped when she swung open Elsie's bedroom door and found not one thing out of place. The blankets were tucked neatly over the mattress and the pillows fluffed and smoothed as if a chambermaid had made her rounds. All the dresser drawers were closed. Even the child's comb, hairbrush, and hand mirror were in perfect order on the nightstand.

Scratching her head at her daughter's sudden neatness, Mrs. Miles plodded down the hall to her own room. After hanging up her husband's robe and pajamas, she suddenly felt very tired. "I guess I'll lay down for a minute," she yawned. "That moving really did me in. I can usually clean all day and not have it bother me."

The next thing Bertha heard was the sound of children's footsteps charging up the staircase. "Oh my!" she cried when Elsie burst into the room and leaped into bed with her. "Are you home from school already?"

"Yes, Mommy."

"An' it looks like Ma was a bad girl," chortled Leo, sticking his head around the bedroom door. "What's Pa gonna say when he gets home an' finds dinner not on the table?"

"Oh, no! I must have slept all afternoon!" exclaimed Mrs. Miles, shaking her head to clear away the cobwebs left from her long nap. "I better get down to the kitchen."

As his mother scrambled out of bed, Leo declared, "Maybe I better help ya, Ma. I don't like chores that much, but they're better than listenin' ta the old man bitch."

"Watch it, mister!" scolded Mrs. Miles. "I need to make more lye soap to wash out that foul mouth of yours."

"Yeah!" chimed the little girl. "You swear like old Uncle Conrad when he and Daddy drank blackberry wine."

"You tell him," laughed Bertha. "Oh, and by the way, Elsie, I want to thank you for picking up your things this morning. You saved me a lot of work."

"What do you mean, Mommy? I slept too long to do anything but get dressed."

"Well, if you didn't tidy up, who did?"

"I don't know, Mommy."

"I do," chuckled Leo mischievously. "Ma was sleepwalkin' durin' her nap an' done that cleanin' without even knowin' it."

"_Did_ that cleaning."

"Whatever ya say, Ma. Let's get supper started. You know how cranky Pa always is after work."

"Bear with your father, Leo. He gets frustrated. Here, he has a degree in engineering and can only find work as a stockboy. Times are hard if you haven't noticed."

"That's why I'm gonna be a prizefighter," promised Boo Boo, shadowboxing his way out of the room. "Then if someone doesn't give me the job I want, I'll beat the daylights out of him."

After the mother and son trooped downstairs, Elsie wandered off to her bedroom. On the way, she saw a moth struggling in a spider web but was too scared to free it. Darting into her room, she slammed the door behind her and pulled a set of jacks from her toy box. Then, she sat on a smooth section of the linoleum floor and began bouncing the little, red ball. After she got the proper height into her bounce, she deftly collected the jacks with a swift, cat-like motion of her right hand. In the middle of her game, she bounced the ball a little high. Just as it reached the apex of its flight, it completely vanished.

Every strand of Elsie's bobbed hair stood erect. Leaping up, she let out a shriek and shot toward the door. Furiously, she yanked on the doorknob, but to no avail. She squealed and pulled and squealed and pulled with every ounce of strength in her frail frame. Elsie continued to tug feverishly until she heard her mother's familiar tread speeding up the hall. Just as help reached her, the door flew open of its own accord, and the terrified girl rushed into Bertha's outstretched arms.

"What on earth is going on?" cried Mrs. Miles, stroking her daughter's quivering shoulder. "What's wrong, child?"

"The ghost took my ball!" wailed Elsie.

"What ball?"

"For my jacks. I bounced it, and it. . .was gone."

"Gone?"

"It disappeared. . .into thin air."

"That's impossible, dear. You must have blinked, and it rolled under the bed or into the closet."

"I don't wanna live in this scary place," bawled Elsie, burying her head in her mother's apron. "Can't we go back to Bradford? Please?"

"But why don't you like it here?"

"This house hates me."

"That's silly," laughed Leo, after sprinting upstairs to see what the ruckus was about. "How can a house hate you? But a brother, on the other hand. . ."

"Are you behind this, Boo Boo?" chided Mrs. Miles.

"No, Ma. My rear's still stingin' from the whoppin' Pa give me for tippin' over old man Zumstein's cow. How was I to know Zummy was on his way out to milk her?"

"Well, then why is your sister so upset if you aren't pulling pranks on her?"

"All girls are scaredy-cats. There ain't nothin' in this old place to worry about, Elsie. I swear."

"But, Boo Boo, you were the one who said a ghost lives here."

"I was just teasin' ya, honest. Why don't ya come down to the kitchen and help us before Pa gets home and gives me another lickin'?"

"Okay. . .Anything's better than playing jacks with a spook!"

The family just returned to the foot of the stairs when Mr. Miles, puffing fiercely on his pipe, blew in the door. "Why don't I smell supper cooking?" he snarled. "What are we having? Baloney?"

"I'm sorry, honey," replied his wife. "I fell asleep before I could get dinner started."

"We could always have cereal, I suppose," grumbled Art. "Afterward, you and I will go get some proper groceries. We didn't bring much food with all the other things we had to lug in yesterday."

"And leave me alone in this spooky, old house?" sobbed Elsie.

"Now, don't start up," scolded her father. "I'm too tired to hear it!"

"Yes, you needn't worry, dear, with your big brother here to protect you," added Mrs. Miles, giving her daughter a loving pat on the head.

"Knowing Boo Boo, he'll give me to the ghost."

"And I'll give you a good paddling," warned Pa, "if you don't stop whining."

"Ease up on the child, Art. She had a real scare today," said Bertha softly.

"Well, she's just going to have to get used to living here!" exploded Pa. "We won't be moving until I get a raise. Heck, I'm lucky to even have a job with the depression in full swing."

Glumly, the family trailed into the kitchen, and Mrs. Miles fetched a bottle of milk from the icebox. She set a pan of water on the wood stove to boil and stirred in some oatmeal. Then, she cut some thick slices of homemade bread with a sharp butcher knife and set out a crock of jam. When Leo reached for a slice of bread, his father scolded, "Not before we say grace, young man. You should know better!"

After dinner, the children did the dishes, while the parents got ready to go to town. As Mr. Miles headed out the front door, he shouted, "I want you kids to go straight to bed now. You need your rest if you're going to do well in school. Especially you, Boo Boo."

Elsie's little hands shook uncontrollably as she thought about braving the shadows creeping up the stairwell. To delay the inevitable, she dropped a handful of spoons she was drying with a dish towel. After they had clattered to the floor, she said to her brother, "Those will need washed again."

"Yeah. Yeah. Or you'll tell Ma. . ."

Dusk had fallen by the time the kids tramped up to their bedrooms. When a wakening owl hooted from the woods out back, Elsie streaked into her room and dove into bed with all her clothes on. She didn't even bother to take off her shoes before burrowing under the covers.

Leo gave Elsie a horselaugh as he watched her worm beneath her bedspread. In a display of false bravado, he stripped down to his skivvies and stood before the bureau mirror flexing his biceps. Then, he struck a series of manly poses he'd seen boxers make before a bout in Bradford. Finally, he crawled under the blankets and propped his head on a pillow to take one last look into the hall.

Suddenly, there appeared on Leo's threshold the silhouette of a tall, thin man with an incredibly wan complexion. The figure was dressed in a dark suit and top hat that reminded the boy of the clothes they buried menfolk in. "Good evening, son," croaked the man through a handlebar moustache. After lifting his hat to reveal a bald head glowing like fireplace coals, he slowly faded into nothingness.

Boo Boo cut loose a scream and scrambled out of bed. Shivering with the chill that had invaded his chamber, he yanked on his clothes and shot across the hall into his sister's room. "Get up, Elsie! Get up!" commanded the lad. "We gotta get outta here! Now!"

"Who. . .was talking. . .to you?" whimpered Elsie, refusing to budge from her bed. "Was that you who just squealed?"

"Never mind! Get up, I say!"

Leo grabbed his sister, still wrapped like a mummy in her blankets, and threw her over his shoulder. He ran down the dark stairs with the radar of a bat and burst into the side yard just as the headlights of his parents' Ford bounced up the rutted driveway.

"What in tarnation is going on here?" shouted Mr. Miles, after braking to a stop. "Is there a burglar in the house?"

"Worse!"

"What do you mean by worse, Leo?" asked his mother, leaping from the car.

"I saw the. . .ghost."

"Ghost, smost," ridiculed Art Miles. "I'll bet this is just another of your fool jokes meant to scare Elsie half to death."

"No. Honest, Pa. I seen him."

"Saw him," corrected Mrs. Miles.

"But I did!"

"S-u-r-e," laughed Leo's father. "S-u-r-e you did. I guess now we'll have to change your nickname from 'Boo Boo' to 'B-o-o-o.'"

"That's a good one, Daddy," giggled Elsie, once her brother set her back on the ground. She wouldn't have been so quick to laugh had she seen the face flickering like lightning in her far bedroom window.

NORTH HALL IS HAUNTED

"They don't call Mansfield a suitcase college for nothing," grumbled Susan, watching her roommate hurry to pack her clothes.

"What's a girl to do?" replied Sherry. "This campus is so dead on weekends that it's just not worth staying here. Why don't you split, too?"

"My parents won't allow it. They say they're paying good money for me to have 'the total college experience,' which doesn't include running back to their house all the time. My father even wants me to sign up for the summer semester."

"Then why don't you visit your Aunt Celia? You're always talking about her. I remember how cool she was at orientation."

"My aunt's special alright. I don't think I'd have gotten through adolescence without her helping me with my problems. But she already invited me for Thanksgiving. I'd hate to impose on her now. She's so busy running her flower shop."

"Well, you could get yourself a boyfriend, Sooze. That'd keep you occupied."

"You know as well as I do that the boys on this campus are pigs. All they do is brag about their sexual adventures. You've heard them! They don't want a serious relationship with a girl. Jerks like that are only interested in one thing."

"But if you got interested in it, too," giggled Sherry, "you wouldn't have to worry about being bored. That's why they keep the TV lounge so dark, you know."

"I'd rather study until my eyeballs fall out than go to the Passion Pit with some hogman. I know what goes on there."

"Then what are you going to do for two whole days?"

"Work on my psych report, I guess. I'm assigned one every month. There sure won't be any noise to distract me with everyone else on our floor leaving."

"Aren't you scared to stay here by yourself after all the stories flying around this week about the ghost?"

"What stories?" asked Susan.

"Boy, you do study too much! The way I heard it, Debbie Weaver went up to practice on the piano in the attic. As she climbed the stairs, she heard someone playing an old ragtime song."

"What's so spooky about that?"

"When Debbie opened the attic door, the music just stopped. And there was nobody sitting at the piano."

"That's creepy alright."

"What's creepy?" asked a surly girl after banging open Susan's door with an overnight bag. "Hurry up, Sherry. We don't want to miss our bus. My Delta Zeta sisters have already left for the terminal and will save us a good seat. I sure hope you pledge our sorority. We'll all love having you as a member."

"I'm almost finished, Barbara. I was just telling Susan about the North Hall ghost."

"The one Debbie heard?"

"You mean you know about the spook, too?" asked Susan with a look of trepidation.

"Sure!" replied Barbara, pulling a red beret over her silky hair. "You must be from Mars if you don't know about her."

"Her?"

"Yeah, the way I heard it, your dorm has been haunted since World War I. My sorority sister told me the story months ago. It seems this lovesick girl got really freaked out after her boyfriend was killed in the trenches of France. She started fooling around with a Ouija board and did all sorts of strange stuff trying desperately to contact him. Her parents, the housemother, and a psychiatrist all counseled her, but she wouldn't listen. One night, after consulting with the spirits, she ran screaming out into the hall and leaped down the stairwell. She fell six flights to the cafeteria in the basement where the security guard found her bloody, dead body. Every freshman class since then has seen her ghost roaming North Hall. And she lived right on this floor!"

"I guess I better keep that Ouija board of mine in the closet, then," tittered Sherry. "I wouldn't want to rile up the spirit world."

"Or your spooked roomie, either," sneered Barbara, noting the hollow look in Susan's eyes.

"Hey, we gotta go, Sooze. See you Sunday night if you haven't shacked up with a cute boy by then."

"Or lapsed into a coma is more like it," mocked Barbara with obvious disdain.

"Get outta here!"

Waving goodbye, Sherry and Barbara shot out the door and merged with a constant stream of freshmen coeds making for the stairwell. The exodus continued for another hour until the sounds of hurried footsteps, swishing skirts, and happy giggles were replaced by a deep, pervading silence.

To escape the ominous hush, Susan closed her door and turned on the radio. The only station that came in clearly was WNTE broadcast by the college. WNTE played a mix of Top 40 hits, and the girl plopped in front of the mirror to brush her hair and sing along to the Beach Boys. "We'll have fun, fun, fun!" she chirped in a breathy alto. "Yeah, right!"

Susan examined her oval face and full lips in the mirror. Why couldn't I get a boyfriend? she wondered. I'm just as cute as Sherry. She's not kidding me. The real reason she goes home every weekend is to see that guy Steven she moans about in her sleep. I got nice long hair that flips up on the end. And straight teeth, too. But why did I have to be born a dumb, old redhead? Everyone knows we're all. . .so temperamental. . .

A sudden knock startled Susan from her reverie, and she leaped up to face the door. "W-W-Who is it?" she stammered. "W-W-What do you want?"

"It's Mrs. Phillips. I need to talk with you."

Susan scurried to the door to admit a tall, brisk woman in her late 50's who served as housemother of North Hall.

The lady stepped inside, and despite herself, checked the neatness of the room before saying, "Sherry Morgan stopped by my office before catching her bus. Like any good resident assistant, she was worried about leaving you up here all alone. Are you going to be okay staying on this deserted floor by yourself? I have a spare bedroom in my suite downstairs if you'd like to room with me this weekend."

"Oh, Sherry shouldn't have bothered you. I'm fine," assured the redhead, imagining the ribbing she'd get from Barbara should she accept this offer. "I'm used to being alone. It's not a problem."

"Are you sure?" asked Mrs. Phillips, noting the strain in Susan's voice.

"Sure!"

"Oh, and I brought you a package."

"Thank you! Why, it's from Aunt Celia!"

"She sends these quite often, doesn't she?"

"Yes. She's my lifeline to the outside world," Susan said.

"Then it must be a care package, dear," smiled the housemother. "Would you like me to walk you down to dinner?"

"Okay. I could try to eat something."

"Be sure to lock your door!"

After turning off her radio, Susan slipped on her tennis shoes and followed Mrs. Phillips down six flights of stairs to the basement cafeteria. There was no activity on any of the floors they passed on the way. The cafe was nearly deserted, too, when the girl bid the housemother "good evening" and got in a short line of ten athletes who were also stuck on campus.

After getting her tray, Susan sat by herself in a corner watching the football players wolf down steaming plates of spaghetti. Ever since she had arrived two months ago, the girl had practically lived on milk. Everything else she found undercooked or burnt to a crisp by the Mansfield food service. Not that her mother's cooking was much better.

Susan glanced at her tray and made a face. Afterward, she snickered under her breath, "The cooks can even ruin Jello. Yuck! They put onions in it. To stay that big, the meatheads on the football team must be eating other food than me. How do they get their necks so thick? They can't even move them to look sideways anymore. Not that they'd notice me, anyway."

Susan nibbled on a piece of Italian bread smeared with rancid butter that made her gag. With a disgusted frown, she picked up her fork and took a bite of salad tainted with hated radishes. When the spaghetti was too soggy to stomach, she got up and dumped the contents of her tray, dishes and all, into the trash bin.

In a huff, the girl stormed outside. She ran down the sidewalk into a wooded park that stretched down the hill in front of her dorm. "My parents must really hate me to have talked me into coming here," she groaned, collapsing on a wooden bench. "So what if Father and Granddad are in the Mansfield State College Jock Hall of Fame? They were too busy scoring goals and kicking home runs to worry about being stuck out in the middle of Pennsylvania's boondocks. The jocks aren't the only animals on this campus. We also have skunks, rabbits, and squirrels."

Susan burst into tears as she glanced at North Hall, the foreboding Gothic building that dominated the center of campus. "I hate my dorm," she bawled. "The towers are straight out of a Vincent Price movie. It's a wonder those windows don't have bars on them. And look at all that ugly, red brick. I swear this place would make a great sanitarium."

The girl covered face with her hands and continued to sob until the long shadow cast by North Hall engulfed her. The sun was close to setting, and a few gray squirrels ran from the trees to dig for acorns before darkness fell. Their chattering roused Susan from her self-pity, and she became aware of a bitter cold that had invaded the late evening air. Shivering, she rose from the bench and trudged dejectedly up the hill toward the cafeteria door.

Back in her room, Susan resumed her disheartening conversation with herself. "I wish I was more like Sherry," she murmured. "She always knows the right thing to say. Everyone loves her to pieces even though she is a tough floor monitor. If she hadn't taken me in after the fight I had with my three roommates on second floor, I would have quit college for sure. I just couldn't deal with sharing a room with that many girls after being an only child. I still can't believe Sherry let a loser like me stay in her R.A. suite."

Susan picked up her psychology text and leafed through it with disinterest. "It's a wonder my case history isn't written up in here," whimpered the coed. "The chapter title could read, 'The Invisible Girl.' That's me. It's like I never existed in high school. I had no dates, no club invitations, no one to notice.

"Even my parents didn't care if I ever left my room. They were too busy sleeping around to pay me much mind. Yeah, they fancied themselves quite the swingers. The way Father strutted around in that smoking jacket, you'd think he was Hugh Hefner. He didn't fool me any. Even a big executive like him couldn't have had that many secretaries. And Mother was just as bad. Every Saturday night she left the house dressed like Zsa Zsa Gabor. When she finally did stagger home, she always reeked of alcohol and strange men's cologne. Eeewww!

"And now that backstabbin' Barbara wants to steal my only friend at MSC. I hate that snob. All she talks about is being a Delta Zeta. If she gets Sherry to join her little clique, I might as well be the North Hall ghost."

The girl slammed down her book and stared bitterly out the dorm window. The lights of the other dormitories glowed eerily through a dense fog that wrapped itself around the hillside campus. Braying laughter floated from the sidewalk below as a few nerds spilled from the closing library across the lane. "I'm so pathetic, I don't even fit in with those kids," sighed Susan. "I might just as well go to bed. . ."

The redhead had just changed into her pajamas when she heard footsteps tramp deliberately up the stairwell and move to the far end of the hall. That, thought the coed, must be one-armed Lefty, the dumb, old security guard, making his rounds. Like he could do anything if there were trouble.

Susan listened intently as the visitor halted before a distant door and knocked twice. After unlocking and opening the door, the visitor closed it again and moved on to the next room. Methodically, the doors opened and closed all down the hall until the footsteps were even with her chamber. Instead of the expected knock, the caller moved past to check the rest of the vacant sixth floor.

Must have seen the light shining under my door, reasoned Susan after the visitor strode by. Maybe I better see who's out there. . .

Working up her courage, the girl slipped on a pink bathrobe and a pair of bunny slippers. Then she crept toward the door and grabbed the knob. The footsteps continued to grow fainter as she fumbled with the lock. By the time she peeped into the hall, the visitor had moved even with the stairwell.

Instead of old Lefty, there floated a misty figure in a baggy-sleeved dress. Her abundant hair was straight on top and curly down the back of her neck. She had on high-topped shoes and dark stockings. Turning, she fixed Susan with a peaceful, dreamy smile. She opened her arms and beckoned with both hands before slowly fading from view.

With a gasp Susan slammed her door and fought to lock it behind her. "A lot of good this will do," she muttered, "when the ghost has the floor key! Why didn't I take up Mrs. Phillips on her offer? Damn my pride, anyway. I get that from Father, the pig."

The girl nervously brushed a stray strand of hair away from her face and then scrambled to turn on her study light. For good measure, she snapped on her roommate's lamp, too. Snatching her Bible from a shelf, Susan withdrew a crucifix Aunt Celia had given her as a confirmation gift and placed it in the breast pocket of her bathrobe. Finally, she collapsed on the bed to think things through.

"It figures that I'd be the one the ghost appears to," ranted the coed. "Scary old Susan, spirit's friend. Too spooky for this world. Too weird to fit in. Thank God for the time I spent with Aunt Celia. She's the only loving person in my whole damn family. Why, I'd better open that package she sent me. Oh, look! She remembered how much I love chocolate chip cookies. Awww! A photo of her and me at the Thousand Islands, New York. We had such fun on that vacation. We shopped, swam, and took the boat tour. Why couldn't Celia have been my mother? She has respect for my feelings. She wouldn't have sent me to this spooky, old college."

Bursting into tears, Susan threw herself on her bed and buried her head in her pillow. After she had cried herself out, she sat up and blew her nose.

"M-M-Maybe I should see what the ghost wanted," mumbled the girl. "Didn't prissy Barbara say a Ouija board lets you communicate with the spirit world? Duh! I should know that. I just wrote a paper for psych class on Ouija boards. I even examined the one Sherry has in her closet while I was doing my research. There. I see it."

Susan crossed the floor and snatched the Ouija board from the top shelf of her roommate's meticulously organized wardrobe. With trembling hands she pulled it out of the box

43

and laid it on her desk. The board had a smiling sun painted in the top left corner with the word "Yes" next to it. In the top right corner was a frowning moon with "No" beside it.

The sun represents the God of the Spirit World, remembered Susan from her report. The quarter phase moon stands for the Goddess of the Spirit World.

Below the two images was the word "OUIJA" spelled out boldly and centered on the board. Under that, all the letters of the alphabet were stretched out in two rows from A to Z. A row of numbers from 1 to 0 came next. At the very bottom of the board Susan found the words "GOOD BYE."

My professor warned against using the board when I chose this topic, reflected the girl, tugging tentatively on her long hair. I even listened to him. But that was. . .before. Even if spirit channeling is a dangerous business, I just gotta try to reach that. . .that ghost. She seemed so happy. Something I want to be. Maybe. . . she. . .can help me. She couldn't be an evil presence, the way she was smiling. . .

Susan picked up the wooden planchette and laid it on the board. The planchette was heart-shaped and had three felt-tipped legs that facilitated its movement. In the center was a plastic window to peer through.

Susan placed her right hand on the planchette. As she deliberately began circling the board with it, she asked politely, "Did I see the North Hall ghost?"

Susan pressed a little harder on the Message Indicator. She moved it faster. Suddenly, the lights began to flicker. A hair brush floated from the girl's dresser and hovered in the air. The girl screamed and let go of the planchette. Her hand no sooner sprang from the heart-shaped object when it moved on its own and spelled out the letters Y E S.

"W-W-Why did you visit me?" stuttered the girl as the brush flew into her hand.

I FELT YOUR PAIN, answered the planchette.

As Susan read the message, the bulb in her

roommate's study lamp flashed wickedly and blew out. Then her psychology text lifted from the desk and began circling her head. Its movement had a hypnotic effect on her, and she asked numbly, "What should I do?"

The textbook dropped into Susan's lap and flew open to the chapter dealing with suicide. Afterward, the planchette moved slowly and deliberately to spell J U M P.

A smile played across Susan's lips. She rose from the bed. After walking rotely to the door, she turned the lock. The door creaked open of its own accord. She stepped into the hall. There, a sudden gust of cold wind mussed her hair and numbed her paling cheeks. She strode transfixed toward a wispy figure standing atop the stairwell railing. The figure smiled invitingly and held out her arms in a gesture of love.

Just before Susan reached the beckoning spirit, a second blast of wind blew her hair across her eyes. When she reached to clear her face, her hand brushed against the crucifix in her breast pocket. The holy cross felt warm to her touch, and she could feel her heartbeat pulsing through it. Images of her dear Aunt Celia popped into her brain with sun-filled afternoons and tall glasses of delicious lemonade.

With a shake of her head, Susan cleared the strands of hair blocking her vision. Clutching the crucifix, she saw the ghost's sweet smile twist into a malicious leer. An expression of self-loathing and total despair revealed the fate that doomed her soul in 1917.

"The damned aren't happy!" cried Susan. "In the name of Jesus Christ, get away from me!"

With a fearful gasp, the ghost recoiled at the holy name. Before Susan could again say "Jesus Christ," the figure lunged forward to snare the coed in its lethal arms. Susan dodged and bolted for the stairwell. In the next instant she was sprinting for all she was worth toward the fifth floor. No lights came on there in response to her cries for help, so she scrambled down and down into the bowels of North Hall. Blindly she ran with a cold wind shrieking at her heels, trying to capsize her. Only her instincts and awakened will allowed her to keep her balance as the wind buffeted her from behind.

Susan descended to the cafeteria just as her churning legs were turning to rubber. She no sooner stumbled into the murky room than a hellish, disappointed wail filled the stairwell behind her. The cold, pursuing wind came to a sudden halt and then sucked upward floor by floor until it vanished in the direction of the attic.

With the last of her strength, Susan crossed the cafeteria, pushed through the hallway doors, and staggered past the vacant TV lounge to Mrs. Phillip's suite. Fighting back the blackness closing around her, she rapped desperately on the smiley face taped to the housemother's door.

The terrified girl tottered at the threshold until a very sleepy Mrs. Phillips answered her flurry of knocks. "I couldn't jump! Couldn't jump!" babbled the coed, collapsing into the housemother's arms. "Help me. Please! Help me live. I want so much to. . .live. To thank Aunt Celia for her. . .love. . ."

HUSBAND (GHOST)

i negotiate
forbidden
space

kinky-haired
she
stretches

lets the sun
caress
her skin

her breasts
feed fantasy
& supple life

i know
i can't
touch her

banished
to starlight
chain gang

THE LATE MR. WILSON

Ask any of my frat brothers. I've never exactly had a reputation for forethought. As a matter of fact, I always rolled out of bed five minutes before my eleven o'clock class and stumbled past the professor still half asleep with the pajama sleeves sticking out of my coat. That inclination also helps explain why I waited until two weeks before the start of the fall semester to enroll in graduate school at Mansfield State College in rural Pennsylvania where I had just spent four years earning my B.S. degree.

By then, naturally, all the decent housing in that small college town was taken. When I discovered that even the dormitories were full, I thought I might end up living out of my car. Just as the situation looked hopeless, I ran into one of my aforementioned brothers who suggested that I visit a boarding house run by a Mrs. Wilson.

Following my friend's advice, I drove up a tree-lined avenue and parked my Ford Maverick in front of a huge, old clapboard mansion. When I rang the doorbell, I was smiling like I expected my fairy godmother to answer the signal. Instead, a ghastly pale women in her late seventies whirred to the door in an electric wheelchair and regarded me with one bright, blue eye. A patch covered her other eye, and her hair was tucked up under a black net. Some of the luster went out of my smile when I regarded her bent figure, but somehow I still managed to inquire, "Is this the Wilson residence?"

"Yes, I'm Mrs. Wilson," replied the woman in a soft, steady voice that belied her infirmity. "May I help you?"

"I-I-I hope so. My friend, Tom Peters, told me that

you rent out rooms, and um--"

"Oh, yes, I remember Tom," the old woman interrupted. "He lived with me two summers ago. He wore wire-rimmed glasses and studied night and day. Tommy was such a nice boy."

"Well, um, Tom, er, said that maybe you could help me out. . ." And before I knew it, I was spilling out my problems to a perfect stranger who sat sizing me up with her one twinkling eye.

Even before I had finished, Mrs. Wilson was backing up her wheelchair and inviting me to "come sit in the parlor." Besides the immensity of the room, one of the first things I noticed was an oil painting that the lady admired periodically as she listened to me rattle on. It depicted a handsome young man in his late twenties. Characteristic of the Jazz Age, his hair was parted in the middle. The portrait had apparently been painted in this very room, for the mantle over which it now hung formed the backdrop for the gentleman's thin build.

"That's a real neat picture," I said when I sat down on an overstuffed sofa opposite my hostess.

"I'm glad you like it," said Mrs. Wilson, obviously pleased. "That was my dear departed husband, Frederick. It was painted during the first year of our marriage by an art professor friend of ours. I must say that it has brought me many fond memories over the years. But then, young man, I suppose that you haven't come here to listen to an old woman talk about such things."

"T-T-That's okay."

"Now. Now. I know in how much of a hurry young people are these days, so let me say that ordinarily I couldn't help you. . ."

I felt my heart sink as Mrs. Wilson paused to catch her breath. She must have noted my crestfallen expression, for there was a hint of kindness in her voice when she continued, "Keep your chin up, son. I only said that ordinarily I couldn't help. You see, all three of my available rooms are spoken for by nice boys who lived here last year.

49

However, because you are a friend of Tommy Peters, and a graduate student to boot, I could let you have my spare room upstairs if you could rustle up a bed and dresser somewhere. Why don't you go up and have a look?"

After receiving instructions from Mrs. Wilson, I charged up the steps to the second floor landing. Directly in front and to the right of me were doorways that opened into the two front bedrooms. To the left was a long, narrow hall. I turned and strode twenty paces down this corridor until I came to the spare room off to the left. Before entering, I noticed a bathroom and a third bedroom farther down the hall.

The spare room was cluttered with Christmas ornaments, tattered furniture, and boxes of old books. Other than that, I really liked what I found. Not only was it twice as large as my bedroom at home, but it also had a large walk-in closet that contained a stairway leading to the attic. It was even on the sunny side of the house and had two windows facing the college. Despite the giant weeping willow that towered just outside, I imagined that there would be a nice view of the campus lights at night.

When I rushed downstairs to tell the dear lady how much I loved the room, her only comment was, "I know the late Mr. Wilson would be pleased to have you as a guest in our home." Then she invited me to stay for tea and plied me with homemade cookies until I thought I would burst. As it turned out, the ten dollars a week I was to pay for rent would hardly have covered all the goodies she would make for her other boys and me.

So began one of the happiest chapters of my college career, or so I thought at the time. After all, what could be nicer than having a third grandmother for a landlady? Come to think of it, Mrs. Wilson was even more understanding than either of my real grandmas. She never got angry when I tracked a little mud into her living room, and she always had an encouraging word for me when I'd stumble into the house after eight hours of research in the library. Even more unbelievable, during hunting season she let me skin squirrels in her kitchen no matter how big a mess I made. Man, what a wife she must have been!

Another nice aspect of living with Mrs. Wilson was the considerate group of guys she had boarding with her. All of them were honor students who spent most of their time studying or sleeping. It was great not having some jerk crank up his Alice Cooper records at three a.m. like in the dormitories. It also worked to my advantage that the other boarders went home every weekend. With a complete catalog of Henry James and William Faulkner novels to read, it was nice that the house got even quieter on Saturday and Sunday. Unfortunately, three months into the semester, it grew stiller than even I could have wanted. It was then, just before Thanksgiving, that the doctors discovered that Mrs. Wilson had cancer and sent her to the hospital for radiation treatments.

About a week after our landlady was wheeled out the front door and loaded into an ambulance, I awoke chilled to the bone. For no apparent reason, Mrs. Wilson's new furnace had died in the middle of the night. I tossed on my pants, a winter coat, and a thick pair of wool socks and scooted for the bathroom. When I peered into the sink and noted all the soap scum and hair that coated its top and sides, I was sorry that I had remembered to brush my teeth that morning. Obviously, Mrs. Wilson's daughter-in-law had been spending so much time at the hospital that she hadn't done our scheduled housecleaning.

Without removing my toothbrush from the rack, I went downstairs and found one of the other boarders smoking on the sofa. His hands shook as, between puffs of his cigarette, he attempted to snip his toenails with a giant pair of scissors he had borrowed from Mrs. Wilson's sewing basket. I might have thought he was shaking from the cold if I hadn't noticed the pasty color of his face.

"Gee, Chuck," I needled as I sat beside him on the couch, "you look like you either chugged a case of green beer or just saw a ghost."

Chuck nodded toward the portrait over the mantle

and then whispered, "Would you believe?"

"Would I believe what?"

"I know this is going to sound crazy, but something really weird happened. D-D-Did you hear any strange noises around two a.m., or so?"

"Heck no! Unless it was the chattering of my teeth. Man, I almost froze to death last night."

"Me, too. I even went down in the basement and tried without luck for an hour to relight the furnace. He must have killed it before freaking me out later on."

"What was it that you heard, Chuck?"

"It wasn't so much what as who."

I glanced sharply at my buddy and found him staring once more at Mr. Wilson's portrait. Chuck's face was etched with worry, and his usually piercing eyes were dull from a lack of sleep.

"What do you mean by that?" I asked. "How could anybody get in here and mess with our furnace when we lock the doors every night before bedtime? You did remember to lock the doors?"

"There isn't a lock built that would stop this guy."

"Come on, Chuck. Will you stop talking in riddles?"

"Okay. Okay," replied my pal, lighting another cigarette. "Let me finish my story and then see what you make of it."

"Go on. Please!"

"Well, the whole thing started a few nights after Mrs. Wilson was taken to the hospital. A couple times earlier this week I was awakened in the middle of the night when I dreamed I heard someone call my name. I was a little spooked each time it happened but always managed to fall back asleep."

"Why didn't you say something before, Chuck?"

"I figured it was just my imagination playing tricks on me with all the stress of finishing my term papers and everything. It wasn't until last night--"

Chuck's voice broke off, and the cigarette shook so violently in his hand that he crushed it out in the ashtray.

Finally, he said, "Last night, as usual, I listened to the Knicks game on the radio. I apparently dozed off sometime in the second half. The next thing I knew, the station was signing off the air, and there was this voice right next to my ear whispering, 'Chuck, Chuck.' I might have thought it was another dream if the light hadn't been on when I opened my eyes. . ."

"What did you see?"

Instead of replying, my friend pointed meaningfully to the portrait of the late Mr. Wilson.

"Yeah, but h-h-he's dead," I stammered as the hairs bristled on the back of my neck.

Chuck smiled weakly before adding, "Maybe you'd better tell him that."

"But what exactly did you see?"

"He was only there for a minute. . .Uh, I mean visible. The face and suit like in the picture, only misty. I blinked, and he was gone."

"Holy smokes!" I exclaimed. "To get a ghost for a roommate is the last thing I need with finals coming up. Now, what are we going to do?"

Before Chuck could reply, a knock resounded through the house that made me leap straight in the air. With a stiff smile Chuck rose quite calmly and went to the front door to answer it. After a moment he returned with a thin coed whose appearance did nothing to allay my own fears. If anything, I became more agitated upon noting her hawk-like face, hoop earrings, and dark, kerchief-wrapped hair.

"Bill, I'd like you to meet Janine."

As I nodded curtly to our guest, my friend added, "She's a psychology major and an expert on the supernatural. I've invited her down to help us solve the mystery I've been telling you about."

Chuck escorted Janine to the sofa and then disappeared into the kitchen. He returned with a tray containing a coffee pot, three cups, milk, and sugar. The girl, meanwhile, was studying the portrait hanging over the mantle. "Who's he?" she asked at last.

"That was Mrs. Wilson's husband," Chuck replied as he poured us each a cup of coffee. Then he proceeded to recount the details of his encounter with that very gentleman to our guest.

The further my friend got into his tale, the more the coffee cup shook on his knee. Finally, Janine took it from his hand and set it on an end table. Afterward, she asked, "When and how did Mr. Wilson die?"

"According to the story I heard," whispered Chuck, "he passed away about ten years ago. He was chopping wood in the backyard and had a stroke. The strange part of it was, he never cried out for help, or anything. He just staggered back into the kitchen, where Mrs. Wilson was making apple sauce, and crumbled dead at her feet."

"He must have loved his wife very much," said Janine thoughtfully. "Did you notice any other disturbances prior to the ones you've been telling me about, Chuck?"

"No, in the four years I've lived here, this is the first time anything like this has happened."

"Yeah, it's funny how as soon as Mrs. Wilson left, things started going to pot around here," I added. "Even the new furnace quit--"

"That's it!" shouted Janine.

"That's what?" I asked nervously.

"The reason for Mr. Wilson's sudden appearance."

"What do you mean?" blurted Chuck.

"Well, look. It's simple. Spirits seldom appear unless they are suddenly troubled by something. Just add up the facts."

"What facts?"

"Mr. Wilson dies ten years ago. Mrs. Wilson stays on here in the house. Suddenly, Mrs. Wilson disappears. She hasn't passed beyond the veil to join her husband in the hereafter, but she's no longer in the house either. This disturbs Mr. Wilson because he loves his wife so much. When she doesn't return after several days, he seeks information. That's why he calls out to you, Chuck."

"But why does he pick on me, Janine?"

"Probably because you've lived here the longest, and he trusts you."

"Great! How can we get him to go away?"

"Well, I doubt if he will until his wife comes home."

"Even if I tell him where she went?"

"I don't think that would help. And besides killing your heat, who knows what other means he might use to show his displeasure over his wife's absence!"

"Other means?" I echoed. "Say, what makes you such an expert on ghosts, anyway?"

"My mother taught me. She's a psychic."

"Oh. . ."

"I-I-I'm sure glad it's Friday," sputtered Chuck. "At least I won't be here this weekend for Mr. Wilson to grill."

"But what about me?" I croaked. "I'm going to be all alone. And with no heat."

"Why don't you go home, too?"

"You know I can't leave, Chuck. I'm out of gas money again, and, besides, I've got too much library research to do."

"Then stay in your room at night," advised Janine. "Just stay in your room!"

That evening, as always, I went straight to the library after supper. Somehow, though, I found the annotated bibliography project that was due Monday a bit trivial compared with the problem of surviving a weekend alone at Mrs. Wilson's. Finally, around seven o'clock I gave up researching altogether. I returned to the house before it got too dark.

By the time I hustled up Mrs. Wilson's front walk, a rising wind whipped the bare branches of the trees lining the avenue. It was getting colder by the minute, and thick snow clouds were powwowing above the roof of the house. My teeth were chattering with more than the cold, however, when I finished fumbling with my key and stepped inside. Just as I flipped on the living room light, the wind slammed the door shut so violently behind me that I about jumped out of my shoes!

55

Averting my eyes from the portrait above the mantle, I dashed to the fireplace and snatched up a poker. Brandishing it before me, I checked the kitchen, Mrs. Wilson's bedroom, and the first floor bath. After snapping on every light on the ground floor, I fled up the stairs and locked myself in my room. Naturally, I gave Chuck's bedroom a wide berth as I scurried past.

Even in my own room I didn't feel safe. As I hung my coat in the closet, I remembered the stairway that led from it into the attic. Quickly, I slammed the closet door and shoved my dresser against it. Then I closed the window blinds and turned on the stereo to muffle the howling wind. Without undressing, I crawled into bed still clutching the poker tightly in my right hand. Naturally, I pulled the covers over my head.

So it was that I must have fallen asleep, for I never heard my favorite song on Santana's <u>Abraxas</u> album before the stereo clicked off. The next thing I clearly recall was jerking awake in a morgue-like silence that was broken periodically by a faint clumping on the front stairs. In a panic I fumbled for the poker, rose noiselessly from bed, and pressed my ear against the hall door. Finally, I heard the muted sound of footsteps disappearing into one of the front bedrooms.

At first, I was too scared to do much more than keep my knees from banging together. It wasn't until the scraping of dresser drawers reached my ears that I remembered Janine's warning about a spirit's "other means" of expressing displeasure. With that thought in mind, I unlocked my door and very cautiously opened it until I could peek down the hall. I nearly fainted when I saw a light shining in Chuck's bedroom. I knew I hadn't turned it on, and it surely hadn't come on all by itself!

It was then that my curiosity got the better of me, and I took a step into the corridor. One step led to two, two to three, and pretty soon I found myself creeping stealthily along toward Chuck's open bedroom door. My palms were so sweaty that I had difficulty gripping the poker I held upraised in readiness over my shoulder. If any further noises had rippled from the room ahead, I hadn't heard them over the pulsebeat thudding through my temples.

As I drew even with my buddy's doorway, a shadow shot out across my path. With a horrific scream, I lunged forward and swung the poker with all my might. Somehow I drew it back just before it struck home in the middle of Chuck's face. At the same instant, his fist froze mid-flight six inches from my head. Tightly gripped in that fist were the deadly, long-bladed scissors from Mrs. Wilson's sewing basket.

I looked at Chuck. Chuck looked at me. The same murderous gleam reflected from our eyes. Finally, my friend's face softened into a smile, and he flung the scissors onto the bed. "If it isn't the late Mr. Wilson," he mumbled.

The next instant we were hugging each other and laughing hysterically. When I finally managed to control myself, I said, "What in God's name are you doing here? I thought you flew the coop with the rest of the chickens."

"I did," grinned Chuck sheepishly. "But I was in such a panic to get out of here that I didn't take the right books with me. With finals coming up, I thought I'd better come back for them. Why did you sneak up on me like that, anyway?"

"Why didn't you yell when you came in?"

"Gee, Bill, I didn't want to scare you."

Again we broke into hysterics while my friend rushed over to his desk and snatched up his chemistry text and a psych book.

"And where do you think you're going with those?" I asked.

"Home, of course."

"And leave me here alone again? Oh, no you don't. I'm going with you."

"What about your research?"

"Believe me. It can wait!"

I ran to my room and tossed a couple of Henry James novels and some clothes in a gym bag. It wasn't until Chuck and I were safely in his car that I realized I again had the poker clutched in my hand. My pal must have noticed it about the same time, for he said, "I hate to disappoint you, Bill, but we don't have any ghosts at my house. Why don't you return that thing to Mrs. Wilson's living room before you hurt somebody?"

"If you go back inside with me and turn on all the lights. . ."

Chuck smiled weakly before shifting into reverse. "On second thought," he muttered, "let's get the hell outta here!"

BLOOD-HUNGRY BEASTS

"This doesn't look a bit familiar," muttered Professor Blaine Richardson, glancing up the dirt trail through a maze of chest high ferns and second growth ash and cherry. "That'll teach me to get such a late start. Guzzling all that vodka with Dr. Williams must have fogged my brain. Man, the last time I came here, I crossed a long meadow by now..."

Fighting back the dry heaves, Blaine collapsed on a log to reflect on his morning misadventures. Although he knew it was a six mile hike to the native brook trout stream he planned to fish that day, he hadn't even crawled out of the sack until 10:30. His queasy stomach had made breakfast out of the question; other than the Coca Cola he had somehow choked down. After gathering up his fly rod, waders, and fishing vest, he had staggered out to his Jeep Cherokee and ground on the starter for a good two minutes before the engine finally sputtered into life. It wasn't until halfway to the stream that he had remembered the fly box sitting on his work bench. That caused even more delay as he did a dangerous u-turn on Route 6 and shot back to his off-campus apartment. By the time his Jeep finally bounced down the old railroad grade to the trail head leading to Doe Run, his stomach was a total wreck. Even worse, the sun had completed half its day's journey toward the East Branch Dam to the west.

As Richardson crawled groggily to his feet, he remembered the old ridge runner who first told him about the wonderful bookie fishing in Doe Run. Blaine had met the gabby fellow at the Creekside Inn after a baseball game. Although the codger was well in his cups, he had warned over and over to always veer right when traveling this trail. "Hell of a place ta git lost," he had slurred by way of conclusion. "Hell of a place. . ."

"Oh, man," groaned Blaine. "I went left at the first fork I came to. That was more than an hour ago. It's too late to backtrack now, or I'll never get to wet a line before dark. This path must hit the stream somewhere, and I just have to try those new nymph patterns I've been working on for so long. Tying them was the only thing that kept my sanity while teaching jerk-off, pilot freshmen all summer. I guess my teaching days are all but over now. Luckily, I still have the woods for a refuge. . ."

With a determined scowl, the fisherman again stumbled up the trail. As he worked his way through the dense woods, he saw not one other boot print in the soft mud beneath his feet. That didn't mean that the path wasn't well-traveled, though, as a multitude of deer tracks keep the grass from intruding onto the lane. There were also plenty of coon prints tipped with impressive claws. Several times what looked like loping dog tracks chased prominently along. "Must be damn coyotes," Blaine said nervously, recollecting the holstered pistol he had left sitting on the kitchen counter by his back door. "Whoever let those varmints loose should be shot! Timber companies most likely were the culprits. They're always whining about the deer ruining the forest. Never did see a doe that could chomp as many trees as a chainsaw. But coyotes? They can eat their weight in fawns and snow-fatigued bucks."

Another hour's hike brought Blaine to the edge of a steep slope leading to a glistening stream below. The downhill path was littered with loose stones that made footing treacherous. The professor held onto his camouflage fishing cap as he skidded most of the way to the bottom. The struggle to keep his balance tested an athletic ability proven on countless ball diamonds and football fields. The murmuring of the brook urged him on until he slid to a halt near its fern-choked bank.

Shivering noticeably, Richardson wiped a clammy sweat from his forehead. "Man, it's getting cold," he said, "and judging by the sun, it can't be more than three o'clock. Sure wish I'd worn something heavier than this canvas shirt. It wouldn't have hurt to bring along a sandwich, either. All that walking cured my hangover and left me hungrier than hell."

The fisherman snapped together his fly rod and threaded the line through the guides. His fingers trembled with anticipation as he tied a hare's ear nymph onto his leader and crept to the edge of the gurgling, freestone stream. Staying low to avoid detection, he flicked the fly with a practiced cast into the current by an undercut bank. The nymph barely hit the water when a dark streak shot out and grabbed it--hard. Blaine set the hook and felt his line tug with a heavy fish. The brookie dove deep and tried to entangle the leader in some roots beneath the bank. Somehow, the angler steered the fish away from the snag and guided it downstream. The brookie splashed and pulled and splashed some more before Richardson was able to yank it out of the water.

"What a fine native," gasped Blaine, admiring the ten inch beauty he had landed. "Look how black he is. That's from living under that bank. If he stayed more in the riffles, he'd be silver. And look at those orange fins and bloodred spots on his side. It's almost a shame to kill such a fish."

Richardson put his thumb in the brookie's mouth and snapped its neck. Then, he inserted the thin blade of his filet knife into the fish's bung hole. He slit its belly up to the gills and removed the innards. Checking the trout's stomach, he found it stuffed with grubs and small insects.

"Looks like flies will do the trick, alright," grinned Blaine. "I'd better stash this fish in my vest and get moving."

The fisherman crept slowly up the stream bank until he came to a place where a log had fallen into the water, forming a deep pool. Richardson had learned from his angler dad that it was best to fish upstream because feeding trout always faced in that direction. Staying below them lessened the chances of spooking the fish. All wild trout were extra skiddish with bears and coons after them, too.

"Yeah, every creature has its natural enemies," said Richardson with a bitter laugh. "Even college profs."

Blaine flicked his fly to the exact spot the current gushed under the log. In an instant he was fast to another brookie, and the fight was on. This fish stayed deep and made slashing runs up and down the pool. It was too large to jerk from the water and too fast to stop.

"Can't horse this monster!" jabbered the angler, frantically feeding out line. "My 4X leader won't stand the strain!"

Expertly, Blaine worked the fish until it tilted exhausted on its side. He slid the brookie onto a sand beach and pounced on it just as the hook pulled free. Before the fish could flop back into the water, Richardson scooped it into his huge paws and found himself clutching a fifteen inch native.

"Wow!" whooped Blaine. "I've never seen a native

this size. Look at that hooked jaw. Maybe I should take the wrong trail more often."

Flushed with excitement, Richardson cleaned his catch and charged upstream hoping for more trophy-sized brookies. His early success made his casts sloppy and his approach less stealthful. Now, he began spooking and losing more fish than he landed. He fell in the stream a couple times, too, and was drenched by the time he finally hauled in his eighth legal trout miles from where he had slid down the slope into this valley.

Blaine flopped wearily to his knees on a mossy stretch of the stream bank. He was weak from exertion and lack of food. He felt dizzy and a little scared when he saw how the shadows had lengthened with early evening.

After peeling off his heavy vest, Richardson reached inside the back pouch and produced a bag overflowing with trout. He laid his catch on the ground and measured each fish with a rusty ruler. With an awed gasp, he counted one fifteen incher, three twelve inchers, three ten inchers, and a nine incher.

"This is the best limit of brookies I ever caught," wheezed Blaine. "Yeah, and I guess I'm equally adept at catching hell. . ."

One-by-one Richardson gave his fish another more thorough cleaning. He inserted his thumb inside each trout and scraped away all traces of the black membrane coating the spine. Then, he ripped out the remaining red gill fragments that could cut a man's fingers to ribbons if he wasn't careful. Afterward, he rinsed his fish in the cold waters of the stream to wash away the slime coating their skin. With a wide grin, he placed the fifteen incher in the bottom of a fresh plastic bag and slid the smaller brookies on top of it.

"That should keep these boys from spoiling," said Blaine. "They're too good eating to waste. The way my stomach's rumbling, maybe I should build a fire and roast them in the coals. I'm going to have to if it gets too dark to find my way out of here."

Weighed down by his heavy catch, Richardson tramped off downstream. His legs felt like rubber, and his eyes had a glazed-over look about them. Thigh-high ferns made the going rough whenever he strayed far from the brook. The stream banks proved equally treacherous. Often, he skidded on the slippery rocks and twice fell on his face.

After a grueling hour's death march, he finally reached the trail leading to the ridge top. Blaine fell four more times on the loose gravel as he struggled up the steep path. His waders had rubbed his feet raw, too. His gait displayed a pronounced limp by the time he struggled to the summit.

The sun was now close to dropping below the horizon, and Blaine still had a long way to walk to reach his Jeep. With renewed urgency, he stumbled up the ridge through the darkening woods. He trudged bravely along, letting his feet find the way. With the evening gloom dogging him, he continued on until he reached the rim of another valley completely unknown to him.

Richardson jerked to a halt and stared down a long incline choked with hemlock. "What the hell?" he muttered. "Must have made another bleeping wrong turn. But where?"

With a weary groan, Blaine did an about-face and limped back the way he had come. Forcing himself to stay alert, he searched in vain for the trail leading to his vehicle. Instead, he ended up where he had begun--on the slope above the stream he had fished all afternoon.

Blaine collapsed and buried his head in his hands. "Stayed too long. Drank too much," he groaned through clenched fingers. "Drank way too bleeping much. . ."

Richardson continued to grumble and curse until the call of a great owl chided him from a shadowy stand of cherry. This hooting filled Blaine with unreasonable anger. Scrambling to his feet, he clambered back down the slope and ran headlong into the thick ferns. With panic jumbling his brain, he raced in circles, not knowing or caring where he ran. Often, he fell or smacked into trees until exhaustion knocked his churning legs from under him.

When the craziness faded from his eyes, Blaine sat up and mumbled, "What to do? What to do? Why, I must be somewhere in Doe Run. Maybe if I go upstream, I'll find the trail I'm familiar with. That will get me back, sure as hell. But how far will I have to walk to get there? Maybe I'd better. . .go downstream. To the East Branch Dam. I'm bound to find someone there. To help me."

A hopeful smile flickered across Blaine's lips. Steadying himself against a scabby-barked cherry trunk, he rose on wobbly legs and staggered off down the creek bank. With darkness closing fast, he used the gurgling voice of the brook to guide him.

Richardson limped tentatively along until a flushing grouse erupted from the ferns. He sprang back in surprise and then dove on his knees to search madly for a baseball-sized rock. Clutching the missile in his hand, he jumped up just as a second grouse took wing. With a low growl, Blaine flung the stone to knock the grouse from mid-flight. Baring his teeth, he leaped on the flopping bird and wrung its neck. "Still got my old pitching arm," he bellowed. "And now I got meat, too. Time to build a fire. Time to eat. You bet!"

In the last glimmers of twilight, Richardson gathered a pile of dry twigs. Urgently, he rifled through the pockets of his fishing vest until he found the matches he had stashed there. The box was soggy from his tumbles into the creek. The first match would not strike on the slick side of it. With trembling fingers, Blaine ruined others on a dew-soaked rock. In desperation, the fisherman struck his last match on the zipper of his pants. The head crumbled before igniting, leaving Blaine to curse his ill luck. Although he could not cook the grouse, he hungrily stuffed it in his vest pouch with his limit of trout.

Gripped again by panic, the fisherman dashed along the creek bank, slashing through patches of ferns and beech brush. His path was now guided by an eerie full moon that rose suddenly over the black hills. The temperature had dropped sharply with the falling of night, and Blaine exhaled clouds of frosty breath as he sprinted downstream.

Finally, Richardson charged from the woods onto a brushy plain. There he encountered a broad dirt road that circled the glimmering waters of the East Branch Dam. With a joyful shout, Blaine danced in the moonlight and raised his arms triumphantly like a victorious marathon runner. "I'm saved! I'm saved!" he blared. "I'll bet this track leads to the new campground the state built on the reservoir last spring."

The fisherman continued to frolic until the foul odor of grouse guts wafted from his vest to choke out his celebration. Turning, he started west up the road only to learn that his panicked exit from Doe Run had turned his feet into a mass of oozing blisters. A searing pain accompanied each step and sent his stomach into fresh convulsions. When his agony became unbearable, Blaine unsheathed his knife and hacked down an ash sapling that grew next to the road. Dropping to one knee, he trimmed off the branches and cut the stout stick to a five-foot length. As he sharpened one end, he said, "This will make a dandy staff. Nothing's going to stop me now."

Richardson rose and started once more up the dirt track. The road led across a meadow and into another dense wood. It became steeper there as it wound along a rocky hillside. Although the walking stick alleviated some of the pressure from Blaine's feet, it could not keep his legs from cramping with the added exertion of the uphill climb. The full moon dipped beneath some clouds, making the going even tougher. With an exasperated groan, Blaine sought shelter in a laurel thicket. Exhausted from his trials, he lay down among the bushes and fell instantly asleep.

Somewhere in his dreams, Blaine found himself in a classroom crammed with unruly students. Although they had college-age faces, they pulled the pranks of junior high brats. Spit wads splatted on the blackboard behind him. A flight of paper airplanes barely missed his face. A fart echoed from a back corner. Boogers flicked from fingers found their mark on a shy, black girl's cheek. "What do ya mean I's gonna fail?" growled a surly voice. "You wouldn't last an hour in my hood, teacha!" An imposing freshman dressed in gangsta leather and a do-rag rose from his desk and swaggered threateningly to the front of the class, waving his red-marked test. He grabbed Blaine's arm and twisted it until the professor's free fist lashed out and bashed the punk square in the mug. The bullying,Tysonesque sneer disappeared in a shower of flying teeth to be replaced by a panel of dour-faced deans. The faces closed to within inches of the accused prof and began clucking in self-righteous judgment. "Professors have rights, too. I had to defend myself!" cried Blaine. "I can't believe you're going to sack me for maintaining order in my own classroom--"

A shiver passed through Richardson. He woke with a start. He crawled freezing from the brush and began pacing stiffly on the moonlit road. His thin shirt had done little to protect him from the frosty night, but that only partially accounted for his trembling. Rubbing his arms to restore their circulation, he growled angrily, "Damn bleeping protocol! Damn it to hell! There wasn't time to call security. Didn't they know that?"

By the position of the moon, the professor could tell it was not yet midnight. He lay down again until the frost-laden air returned him to his pacing. "No wonder I stayed too long and drank too much," he grumbled after scrambling from the laurel. "Punks are punks no matter what color they come in. Trustees say we must save our inner city youth. I don't have a problem with giving these kids a chance. . .but not an unfair advantage. Yeah, and just how much will they learn if bad grades or behavior can't fail them? I'm no babysitter. Screw the summer pilot program! And screw the university sponsoring such a beast! I still can't believe that gangster's strutting around campus instead of behind bars where he belongs. Man, I was the one who was assaulted."

Richardson lay down a third time. He just began to doze off when a haunted howl echoed from the trees near the reservoir. Moments later, it was answered by a closer baying above him on the ridge. Soon, a third howl emitted up the road behind him.

Stealthily, Blaine rose from the bushes and slipped

back onto the trail. Using his walking stick to great effect, he worked his way in the direction of the camping area he hoped was not far. The moon popped from the clouds to bath the woods in an otherworldly glow. Often, the fisherman caught glimpses of the shimmering reservoir just off to his left. He continued to hobble along until he heard the excited yips of a pack of coyotes gathering close to where he had bedded down. With fear surging through his veins, Richardson broke into a painful gallop.

The dirt track climbed steeply upward before leveling off at the next hillside bench. A few yards ahead, laurel flanked the road on both sides, forming an eerie, black tunnel. Blaine didn't want to be trapped there of all places. Afraid his fly rod would get tangled in the bushes, he flung it aside. He darted forward again just as a pack of slathering canines came bounding up the road toward him.

Why in the hell are they after me? asked Richardson's brain as he streaked as fast as his blistered feet would allow. I thought they were afraid of humans. But then freshmen aren't supposed to attack their professor, either. Has this whole bleeping world gone crazy? Can't those coyotes catch my man's scent by now?

No! screamed his instincts. Not with that grouse still in your vest. Run, man. Run!

With the coyotes snarling at his heels, Blaine rushed up the laurel tunnel into total darkness. The excited yips and snapping of sharp teeth made him dash faster than any track opponent he had raced against in his prime. Finally, he broke into the open woods where the moon's floodlight glare revealed a ghastly sight. There, just a few yards ahead him, he discovered that the trail ended at the edge of a steep precipice.

"So much for finding that campground," croaked Blaine. "I-I-I'm on a bleeping fire road."

Richardson skidded to a halt inches from the brink of a hundred foot drop into the reservoir below. With beads of fear glinting on his forehead, he gaped into the chasm. The lead coyote, drunk on blood lust, wasn't as lucky. Off it shot into nothingness, ki-yiing fearfully as it plunged to its death. Richardson whipped around and thrust his walking stick like a spear just as the second coyote lunged for him. The force of the beast's leap drove the stick deep into its chest, and it fell thrashing to the ground. Moments later, it too flopped over the cliff, leaving four more snarling curs to content with. Blaine yanked out his filet knife and slashed madly at the next bold beast. A lucky swipe lopped off the end of the coyote's nose, and it turned and fled back into the laurel.

The last three canines attacked in unison. Blaine dodged at the last second, and the curs sprang past him and on over the cliff to join their dispatched kindred. With a victorious whoop, Richardson turned to leave the brink of the precipice only to find his path blocked by the wheezing, wounded coyote. With moonfire glittering in its eyes, the beast leaped at the professor and planted its fangs in his thigh. Blaine dared not back up. Grabbing his antagonist by the ears, he dove on top of the coyote and wrestled it savagely to the ground.

Back and forth the man and beast rolled, with neither able to gain advantage over the other. Blaine's limbs streamed with blood as he buffeted the coyote with his hammer-hard hands. The animal slashed with its fangs, oblivious to the heavy blows pummeling its back and flanks.

Finally, in desperation, Blaine latched onto the coyote's throat. The beast kicked and rolled in a mad repeated motion, but the man would not loosen his grip. With all the energy it could muster, the coyote pitched toward the cliff, dragging the professor behind it. Snarling viciously, Richardson throttled the beast until its windpipe popped. As he tried to untangle himself from his suffocating enemy, he felt the rocky soil of the cliff dissolve into rushing air.

Hurtling toward the water below, Blaine thought about the fork he had missed in the trail. There wasn't much for him to return to, anyway. Drinking too much and staying too long was just as much a part of being a man as standing up to coyotes and punks in do-rags. He closed his eyes as he felt the frigid wind numb his senses. The waves heaved up to greet him. Then there a black silence devoid of the slathering jaws of deans, trustees, and other blood-hungry beasts.

THE GOOD SHIP <u>DEATH</u>

Impressed by mist,
the good ship <u>Death</u> sailed
close-hauled and harried.
Icebergs loomed
on every tack,
and walruses bellowed
from invisible islands.
Watchmen cursed,
cabin boys blubbered,
and bosuns' pipes squealed
like scalded demons.
Old salts sweated
in the rigging,
praying for passage
to the aurora borealis.

JIM MORRISON

Jim Morrison created an organ-mad world
where spooky sideshows churned
to a Whiskey a Go Go beat.
His leather pants housed love/death drama,
while Indian beads completed his mystique.

Jim had the face of a troubled angel,
the voice of a banished one.
He drowned the stage in his anguish,
unleashed a vision of social rot
& emotional wilderness of stone.

Morrison was a satyr & an oracle bard.
He chanted tales of homicidal hitchhiker
& unknown soldier blood meal.
He used his words like a conqueror deploys
troops.
He dared confess that we are ruled by television.

Jim Morrison was a stoner lord
who took his toke of life & OD'd on it.
He died naked in a Paris tub,
freed from the eyes
that vaporized his star.

CAN YOU GIVE ME SANCTUARY

Bobby Fredericks' parents were at it again. He could hear them rumbling at each other through his locked bedroom door like two warring thunderheads. Lately, their squalling had become a nightly ritual. It seemed that the smallest thing would set them off. Planning next evening's dinner menu, rooting for different contestants on <u>The Price Is Right</u>, or bickering over the last beer in the fridge, inevitably ended in an all-out screaming match.

"Oh, well," the boy sighed. "Still one place to go. Still one place to go."

Bobby leaned over, flicked on his lamp, and then crawled out of bed. Crossing the room, he stopped in front of an antique bookcase that sagged beneath the weight of an incredible rock 'n' roll album collection. These records provided the boy with much more than a pleasant pastime. Over the years they had become his panacea and religion. Their power chords pumped up his confidence, and, on nights like this, they formed a shield against the horrible howl of his parents' altercations.

Of all the albums in Bobby's collection, it was those of the Doors that he held in special reverence. Unlike his friends, he had not bought the records to be cool. There was something about the group's eerie, organ-mad music that spoke of eternal sadness. What really hooked him, though, were Jim Morrison's tormented vocals. Every time he heard the singer's anguish, Bobby knew that there was someone else who understood why he locked himself in his bedroom every night.

Bobby was introduced to the first Doors' LP at a

73

stoner party he attended. He had only gone to defy his father, not because he smoked weed. Even before he heard one note of the record, he was totally enthralled by the cover art--a photo of the musicians' blank, staring faces superimposed on a dark background that shrouded them in total mystery. By the time the radio staple, "Light My Fire," blasted from the speakers, Bobby had already heard five incredible songs dripping with sex and dark imagery. It was "The End," though, that voiced the same growing alienation that was eating at the very core of his being. The song wove in and out of his head for eleven minutes and thirty-five seconds as Morrison unraveled a stark tale of Oedipal lust and mayhem. Its psychological stream-of-consciousness mind trip was the most powerful experience of Fredericks' young life.

After that, the release of each subsequent Doors' album became a major event to Bobby. He would haunt the local record shop for weeks until it finally arrived. Then the record would remain on his turntable until he could growl out the lyrics to each song verbatim. It was after he had so digested the Doors' second album, <u>Strange Days</u>, that the boy let his hair grow down to his shoulders. He also bought his first pair of leather pants. Morrison's vision of the sinfulness and unreality of life had won him a new disciple in spades.

<u>Waiting for the Sun</u>, though, was the LP that sent Fredericks into a downward spiral as his fixation on the Doors became complete. Many songs on the record contained messages of overt revolution and sensuality that impacted Bobby's personality. "Hello, I Love You" ignited an obsession with two young hippie chicks that he leered at every day at school, aching for wild, debauched nights of sex and discovery that Morrison himself so reveled in. Then "Yes, the River Knows" fueled a drinking problem Bobby only concealed by withdrawing further from his family. When his father started in on him about his appearance or strange behavior, the boy would scream out the words of "Five to One" and bolt from the dinner table. Morrison's politically charged lyrics no longer allowed Bobby to tolerate the older

generation's power trip. It was after one such act of open rebellion that Fredericks began wearing a single strand of Indian beads around his neck in emulation of his shaman--Jim.

Tonight Bobby's sadness went much deeper than usual. He turned off his lamp and plugged in the black light that hung over his bed. His wall-to-wall Doors' posters sprang instantly to life. In their ghostly, phosphorescent glow, he selected the <u>L.A. Woman</u> album from his collection and slid it carefully from its protective sleeve. As he placed it on the turntable, he made sure not to smear greasy fingerprints on the grooved vinyl. To do so would have been like tearing a page from a holy text.

Bobby cranked up the volume until the walls began to shake. He still couldn't believe that Morrison was gone! None of the facts of his death made any sense. How could the Word Man have had a heart attack while relaxing in the bathtub? How could anyone be sure that he was even in the coffin they buried at Pere La Chaise Cemetery? After all, only his wife Pamela and the mysterious doctor who signed Jim's death certificate had actually seen the body.

Bobby lay back on his bed and let the music wash over him. As he chanted along to the guttural blues of "Been Down So Long," he thought the words had never seemed more appropriate. Gripped by the powerful vibe, the boy leaped to his feet, his clenched fists upraised. Then he snatched a pool cue from the corner and wielded it like a microphone stand when "L.A. Woman" exploded into his consciousness. He continued to writhe trance-like in perfect imitation of the Lizard King until the hot, hypnotic rock faded from the room.

Bobby turned the album over, flopped back on his bed, and closed his eyes. There was an angry rapping on his bedroom door, but it seemed somehow very far away. He lapsed into a dreamy reverie until the piano intro of "Riders on the Storm" rippled from the speakers. The boy still did not open his eyes until Morrison's voice did not come bursting into the mix where it should have. It was as if someone had erased the vocal track from a song Fredericks had heard hundreds of times before.

Bobby propped himself up on one elbow and stared through the eerie glow of the black light posters at his turntable. It was a Dual of the latest design and was equipped with a dust cover made of smoked plastic. Rising from the spinning disc beneath was a human head.

The face stopped rotating and became more distinct. It completely filled the space beneath the dust cover. The "Riders on the Storm" instrumental track continued to play as Bobby blinked in disbelief at the oh-too-familiar shock of brown hair and vacant, bulging eyes. The other features were as youthful and angelic as they had looked in 1967.

"Jim! Jim!" Bobbie gasped.

"It's hip here, man," replied the face after a moment.

"W-Where are you? You're supposed to be d-d-dead. . .or in Africa."

"On the other side of morning. . ."

"The. . .what?"

"Don't have to put up with a bunch of bullshit here, man. Don't have to stay loaded to make the scene. No hangups about sex, nakedness. . ."

"What about parents?"

"My old man, the admiral, would never make it here. Yours, either. Dig?"

Suddenly, the pounding on the bedroom door grew louder and more insistent. Each rap was punctuated with the incoherent raging of Bobby's father. In a daze the boy rose to his feet. Lurching toward his turntable, he muttered, "Jim. Jim! Can you give me sanctuary, Jim?"

"Sure, man. . .Just lift the dust cover. . .I'll help ya, man."

As Bobby approached his stereo, the music engulfed him. It took all of his strength to obey his shaman's command. Then, it was as if Morrison's voice echoed from the boy's own being. He never heard his father kick in the bedroom door. He stood transfixed, humming madly, watching the Elektra butterfly on the record label spin around and around. . .

THE ELEMENTARY LIBRARIAN

The elementary librarian
lurked in a maze
of Gothic book racks.
Her step was a whisper,
and her presence dour
as a tombstone.
Sweat seeped from her
greasy, gray locks
and down a neck
waxy with witch's tallow.
We feared her worse
than a paddle's crack.
Her talons were the envy
of the Grim Reaper.

MRS. BABCOCK'S ABC'S

It was late afternoon, and pudgy Perry Black sat alone in his second grade classroom. Even the casual observer would have seen he was scared. His red freckles stood out like chicken pox on his pale cheeks, and his hands twisted nervously in his lap. His teacher sure was taking her time returning from the principal's office. Knowing her sadistic tendencies, the boy figured that was all part of the punishment.

Perry stared at the wall clock above the door and saw that it was 3:22. He heard the last of the buses rumble out of the parking lot. Once they were gone, an eerie silence crept over the schoolyard. Inside, the building was even quieter. The prisoner squirmed listening to the distant rattle of the furnace pipes below him.

Now, my parents gotta pick me up, an' school ain't the only place I'll be in trouble, Perry worried. Our farm's far out in the country, and Pa sure hates quittin' his chores to drive way into town. This time I'm gonna get a whippin' for sure.

Perry's nose wrinkled in disgust while he pondered the source of his trouble--Mrs. Babcock. "What a nasty, old witch she is, anyway!" he grumbled under his breath. "If she ain't rippin' on me with that sharp tongue of hers, she's rappin' my fingers with a ruler. Even worse, she gives me so much homework, I can't play Peewee Baseball. I still don't see why Ma thinks 'rithmetic is more important than smackin' long home runs. There's no dang escape from Babcock's torture."

The boy also hated how dark his teacher kept the

room. She never let in any sunshine. Last week she clawed him good when he tried to open the blinds and show her a rainbow he'd seen during recess. Now, the light was so dim, he could barely make out the print of the Dick and Jane book he was assigned to finish. He was behind a grade in reading as the hag was constantly reminding him.

There's no way to get back at old Babcock, either, the boy reflected. She never sits down without checking her chair for tacks. An' crap! She actually <u>likes</u> the snakes an' toads I put in her desk. I'll bet she makes soup out of 'em. Yeah, and it only made her laugh the time I yanked out my loose tooth an' dribbled blood on her new pantsuit. I wiggled the tooth <u>all</u> day so I could pull it out when she bent over to get my math test after sixth period. Wow! Did she get excited seein' my blood. That was creepy!

Today, in desperation for revenge, the boy had attempted to slip a rotten apple into Mrs. Babcock's lunch sack while she was in the hall gossiping with another teacher. The apple was so decayed that even the pigs wouldn't eat it. If his classmates hadn't burst out laughing, he'd have gotten away with it, too.

"All the sixth graders say Mrs. Babcock's a ghoul," mumbled Perry. "That's why she always comes to school before daylight and goes home after dark. But who can believe them? Sixth graders will say anything to scare a little kid. They also told me the principal sleeps in a coffin down in the basement."

Perry looked in his desk and took a quick inventory of his cache of weapons. There were two spit wad straws, a rubber band gun, and three bobby pin snappers. These might keep away Dan the bully, he thought, but they sure won't protect me from that crone--Babcock.

The boy continued to dawdle until the sound of hurried footsteps reverberated from the hall. By the time his teacher entered the room, Perry's nose was once again buried in the first grade reader. He had perfected his fake study techniques so he could even fool his mother. He felt he could carry this off long enough to be sent on his way home.

Mrs. Babcock glared balefully at her student. Seeing he was holding his book upside down, she screeched, "Dick and Jane would run much faster if they weren't standing on their heads!" To drive home her displeasure, she pinched Perry's fat cheeks before returning to her desk.

Reddening, Perry flipped over his text and hid behind the cover. Even reading was better than looking at his teacher. Not only was she tall, gaunt, and ugly, but the lad hated how her bones showed through her transparent skin.

"Perry!"

The boy sat up with a start and found Mrs. Babcock scrutinizing him. It gave him the willies the way she kept staring at his fat arms. Now, I know how the Thanksgiving turkey feels when Pa inspects its drumsticks before deciding whether to cut off its head, Perry thought.

"What's the matter with you, boy?" snarled the teacher. "You haven't turned a page in five minutes. Have you forgotten how to read, or are you hatching another of those schemes of yours?"

"I ain't doin' n-n-nothin', ma'am," stuttered Perry.

"That's obvious," croaked the cadaverous woman slyly as she yanked open her desk drawer. "I think it's time we reviewed our ABC's."

"A-A-ABC's?" bleated the scared lad.

"Yes, my devious, little fellow, A is for apple."

Perry swallowed hard as he watched Mrs. Babcock produce the piece of decayed fruit that he had tried to slip into her lunch bag. She took a bite out of the rottenest spot and then sucked a worm from the core like it was a strand of succulent spaghetti. After licking the brown slime from her lips, she said, "And B, of course, is for boy--a plump, tender boy for supper!"

Perry leaped up screaming and bolted for the door, only to find Principal Thomas blocking his exit. The towering man smiled broadly to reveal a mouth full of sharp, yellow fangs.

From behind Perry echoed Mrs. Babcock's screeching laughter. "And then there's C," she cackled, rising menacingly from her desk. "I'll bet even you can guess what that stands for."

Perry glanced warily at his teacher and shook his head, "no." Then he dodged back into the classroom just as the principal lunged to grab him.

"<u>Crimson</u> is the answer you're looking for," Mr. Thomas thundered, while he and Mrs. Babcock backed Perry into a corner. "Crimson is the color of blood. Warm, tasty human blood."

THE RATCATCHER

The ratcatcher entered the morgue sewer
in search of more meat for his traps.
As he slunk along the tunnel,
his torch cast furtive shadows
and illuminated bold, red eyes.
The man rearranged his bulging pack,
pulled closer his rat-clawed cloak.
The reek of decay penetrated his flesh.

Finally, he reached a grated gate
which he opened then locked behind him.
Here the rats were more plentiful
and paid no heed to a torch thrust.
Entranced herds rushed by in droves,
leaping up and over the ratcatcher's legs.
Soon he was buried under a high tide of rats
caught in the throes of panicked flight.

Once they had passed, the dazed man
rose sputtering from the slime,
shaking tangled rats from his cloak.
There before him tottered
a half-rotted corpse
whose cheeks bulged, obscene with chewing.
Slimy tails dangled from an O-shaped maw
then disappeared like strands of spaghetti.

As the ratcatcher backed fumbling
toward the locked gate behind him,
he barely felt the trapped rodent
biting him through his cloak pocket.
He smashed it with a quick blow of his fist
then immersed his fingers in squishy blood.
He only hoped he could retrieve his key
before the cadaver was upon him.

TRAPPED

Robert Williamson was a solitary man and a painter known for his meticulous workmanship. His eye for detail is what had won him the job as caretaker of the Weir Apartment Complex. He was summoned by Weir's manager after a particularly slovenly couple had moved out, leaving their flat stained and battered.

The painter thought the old renters must have been named "Nailor" after spotting the picture hangers they had hammered everywhere in the walls. With a chuckle at his own wit, Robert began pulling the nails and spackling the unsightly holes. He also sanded off crayon marks and washed away dirt smudges with a damp rag. Moving systematically from room to room, it took him eight hours to do the necessary prep work.

On the second day Robert returned to begin painting. He cut in along the edge of the walls and around the window frames with careful strokes of his brush. Using the standard off-white paint prevalent in the Weir Complex, one rolled coat was all that was needed. He had chosen an eggshell finish, which was known to hide flaws in less than perfect surfaces.

Whistling and grinning, Williamson zipped through the living room and the first of two bedrooms by early afternoon. There was one detail he overlooked as he entered the second chamber. It wasn't until he shut the door behind him that he noticed someone had removed the handle. The latch shot home with an evil snick, and the painter found himself trapped in a tiny, square, six yard space.

Fighting back panic, Robert removed the hinge pins

from the solid oak door. Although he reefed with all his might, it wouldn't budge. Then he beat frantically on the bedroom walls, hoping a neighbor might hear. After stomping on the soundproof floor proved equally futile, the workman felt a worried sweat soak through his bib overalls.

Robert yanked open the window facing the railroad yard out back. With an urgent yowl he hurled "Help" against the hissing of steam engines and the clanging of sledgehammers on metal. He yelled until his throat was raw and then yelled even louder. It wasn't until his vain pleas triggered a hungered scratching from inside the corner closet that the painter knew the true meaning of "claustrophobic."

THE SENDING

The wizard repaired to the graveyard
and began digging like a crazed gopher.
His cape glowed in the moonlight
with an eerie phosphorescence
that made his movement stutter.
He only slowed when his shovel hit wood.

He mumbled a malefic incantation
and then extracted the coffin
like a rotted tooth.
The lid gave way with a shudder,
and the wizard bent to lick the froth
from the corpse's mouth and nose.

He forced a drop of his own blood
down the decayed throat,
and when the coffin lurched to life,
he leaped to subdue his new Sending.
This was the liveliest one yet.
He taught it to hunger for his enemies.

REJECTIONS

My name is Jazz James. I'm the editor of a leading East Coast horror mag. Gimme a break, man. I only accepted this gig to make a fast buck. I didn't even mind all the weirdos I had to put up with. That is until about a year ago when I began receivin' some real sick fiction from this dude named Scully Graves. Man, the only thing remarkable about his stories was the queer scrawl in which they were written. Not that typin' the mothers would have helped much.

The cat did have a way with gore, though. It like got to be his signature. First, he sent me this story about a satanic rock singer who broke a blood vessel in his throat and choked to death performin' on MTV. It was a real turkey. No character development. No major theme. No nothin'! Then there was the one about the freaked-out wino who went to sell some blood and ended up drinkin' the Red Cross dry. Later, he even sent me a tale about a Latin American dictator who got his jollies executin' political prisoners each mornin' to "procure" blood for his daily bath. Yuck! It seems like the more of Scully's stories I rejected, the bloodier the mothers got. Before long, he was submittin' a story a week, and I was sendin' 'em back just as fast.

Finally. . .uh, last month it was. . .UPS brought me a package. The sucker was about twenty inches square and wrapped in this sticky stuff that kinda resembled fly paper. Although it had no return address, I knew it had to be from old Scully. That wasn't too hard to figure out 'cause my name and street number were written in that same queer, familiar scrawl as all the other crap he'd ever sent me. Oh well, at least about that same time, those god-awful stories of his quit comin'.

Needless to say, gettin' that package really had me freaked! I kept turnin' it carefully over in my hands wonderin' what was inside. Could it be a whole new batch of sicko stories? Could it be a gross, bloodlettin' novel that he wanted me to serialize? Gag me, man! I just didn't have the stomach to open it. I had enough problems of my own then with my old lady packin' her bags, an' all. Can you believe she said I was insensitive? Me?

Well, anyway, havin' that package around kinda ate at me after a while. You know, like that present your ma would hide in the closet before Christmas. God, I musta picked it up an' rattled it a few thousand times before I finally tried to tear it open. That was a few minutes ago. You'd think I'da known better. Especially after I'd dulled two knives an' a pair of scissors tryin' to peel that sticky skin off the outside.

What a perverse dude old Scully is. Can you believe that he sent back all my rejection slips? What a worm! What a--

Hey! What's that red gorp bubblin' up from the bottom of the box? Hey! Get off me! Hey!

If my writin's become hard to read, it's 'cause I'm now usin' my left hand. My right arm is totally useless. Man, is it swollen. Twice as big as normal. It looks like it's gonna bust. An' fluid's leakin' from my elbow an' wrist. Talk about throb! Ow!!

Yeah, an' his flesh eatin' bacteria keeps spreadin'. Like crazy. Scully called it "necrotizing fasciitis." In his very last story I rejected. Warn my replacement. If ya got the stomach to look at what's left of me. An' find this letter. . .

YOU (POLTERGEIST)

You are the scent
of nicotine and damp earth.
Frostily you glide
through the mortuary wall
to recreate your karma.
You're slippery as eel skin
and just as dark.
Your dreams do not perish.
Your hatred is as concrete
as objects smashed
through telekinesis.

EDGAR'S VACUUM

Holding a wastebasket at arm's length, the brisk old woman approached her husband. The bald duffer continued to shuffle back and forth absently vacuuming the living room carpet until she stepped directly in his path. Seeing the fire shoot out of her eyes, he reluctantly flipped off the sweeper. Then he hung his head guiltily and pretended to examine a worn spot in the rug. This infuriated his wife even more, and she shoved the trash container under his nose. The unmistakable odor of human feces immediately invaded his nostrils, backing him against the wall.

"Edgar! Why do you do these things? I swear that between you and Kitty I'll soon be a nervous wreck. First, I find that Kitty hasn't been using her litter box again, and now this! Can't I leave you two alone even for a few minutes while I go shopping? Why do you plague me so in my old age? Bless my soul! What would our son say if he came home first and found this?"

Avoiding his wife's gaze, the old man pulled at the buttons of his faded cotton shirt. His arthritic left hand picked its way across his chest and then scratched at his right ear.

"And by the way," nagged the old woman, "why did you change your clothes again? This is the third time this morning. Just look at the cockeyed way that you've buttoned that shirt. Can't you do anything for yourself anymore? Did you remember this time that the flap is supposed to go in front of your undershorts?"

Finally, Edgar's wife lowered the wastebasket, wheeled around, and stalked back into the kitchen. As she stormed out of the room, she couldn't resist kicking at a loose-skinned, white cat that disappeared under the sofa with an agility that belied its great age.

When the old woman had gone, Edgar stumbled forward, tripping over his untied shoelaces. His hands did not stop trembling until he had once again switched on the vacuum cleaner and felt its motor respond to his touch. Cooing vaguely, he began stroking the dust bag, which extended full-length down the back of the upright machine. As he caressed it gently, almost lovingly, he detected a slight surge of the engine. Stooping with great difficulty, he placed his ear close to the bag before massaging it again. This time there could be no doubt of the increase in power produced by his touch.

While Edgar listened to the revving of the vacuum motor, his eyes grew misty with remembrance. In a rare coherent moment he suddenly saw himself back in his body shop tuning the engine of a Model A Ford it had taken him years to restore. Oh, how he had loved to tinker with that car! He remembered buying it for fifty dollars from an old woman who must have never changed its oil. When Edgar rescued the Ford from the dilapidated barn she had kept it in, the bearings were burned out, and squirrels had built a nest under the hood. It was only through my loving care, thought Edgar, that I was able to bring that fine machine back to life. If it wasn't snowing out today, I'd take it for a little spin right--

"Edgar!"

The old man started from his reverie at the shrill sound of his wife's voice and found himself face-to-face with someone he would rather not have seen. It was his hairdresser son back from the big city where he now owned a whole string of salons that catered to fellows of his kind. And he hadn't changed a bit. He was still tall and thin with pouting lips and droopy eyes. A dark wave of neatly-styled, shoulder-length hair accented a wan complexion and finely-chiseled features more befitting a fashion model than a young man of twenty-five.

"Hi, Faaa-ther," Roger squeaked above the roar of the vacuum.

Instead of answering, Edgar stared dully at his son, who took a dainty puff from a filtered cigarette poised between two neatly manicured fingers.

"Edgar! Are you going to stand there like a dolt?" shrieked his wife. "I don't believe you have a mind anymore. There must be a vacuum inside that head of yours. Didn't you hear? Maybe if you'd turn off that blessed machine, you'd recognize the voice of your only son. Isn't he just as handsome as ever? And just look at that sharp suit. Why, you're absolutely dressed to kill, Roger."

Edgar's eyes traveled from his son's saddle shoes to his three-piece white suit before reluctantly flipping off the vacuum. The "hello" died on his lips, however, when he noticed the faint hint of mascara that highlighted the young man's unusually thick eyelashes.

When Edgar still did not answer, his wife glared at him and then took her son by the arm. "Never mind, Roger," she said. "Don't mind an old man in his dotage. Come along, and I'll show you to your room. It's just the way you left it. Come along. Come along."

As the mother and son disappeared up the stairwell at the far end of the room, Edgar wondered how his son managed to keep his hands so clean. Why, he couldn't recall when his own fingernails weren't either caked with grime or garden soil. Usually, he had to wash his hands four or five times before his wife would allow him to sit down to supper. Then, afterwards, when the dishes were cleared away, he was right back at the kitchen table tinkering with some gadget and resmearing himself with grease. He could still vaguely remember adjusting an antique cuckoo clock. Then another time it had been this very vacuum cleaner that had gone on the blink--

"Edgar!"

The old mechanic looked up just as his wife and son reappeared in the stairwell. He could tell that the woman was absolutely livid by the stateliness of her manner. She always puts on the dog when she's nervous or angry, reflected Edgar. That's the thing that first attracted my attention back in 1910, or was it 1913, when she was crowned homecoming queen. The only reason I scored three touchdowns was because Jenny and her court were seated behind the end zone. . .

When the old man's eyes unglazed, he saw that his wife was shaking a closed fist just inches from his nose. Finally, she opened her hand and revealed a small mound of bird seed.

"Edgar! Do you have any idea how <u>this</u> might have gotten into our son's bed? It just didn't fly up there by itself! Imagine my surprise when I turned back the covers and found <u>this</u>! I ought to turn you over my knee and--"

Although the old man braced himself for the worse, he never learned what that might be. Just as his wife was about to announce his punishment, the vacuum cleaner clicked on and grew louder with each word she uttered. By the time she had reached over and turned off the machine, she was so totally beside herself that she could do little more than threaten him with a wagging finger.

"Now, that was totally uncalled for, Faaa-ther," drawled Roger. "How vulgar of you to activate that contraption just when Mother was about to chastise you for your boorish prank."

"But I didn't turn on--"

"Just like you didn't spread bird seed in my bed, I suppose. Don't lie. Mother and I both know you did it. Why don't you put that piece of junk down in the cellar with the rest of the tras--"

Before Roger could finish, again the vacuum clicked on, drowning out his squeaky voice. In a fit of anger, the young man lashed out at the machine. There was a bright flash, a shower of sparks, and a squeal of pain that had the old woman leaping forward to save her only boy. After struggling vainly with the off switch, which was stuck, she dove behind the machine and unplugged it from the wall.

"That nasty thing bit me," whimpered Roger when

the roar of the motor had died from the room. Feigning a swoon, the young man collapsed onto the sofa, and Kitty immediately scrambled from beneath it and leaped into his lap. "Filthy, shedding beast," he shrilled, pushing the cat roughly to the floor. "I was almost killed, and now I'm subjected to picking cat hair from my new suit."

"Never mind, dear," cooed the mother. "I'm <u>so</u> sorry about the shock you got. Your father must not have properly rewired the sweeper the last time he rescued it from the scrap heap. The darn, old thing shorted out when you touched it. Now, run along like a good boy and bring in the rest of your luggage. It will take your mind off everything."

Sucking on his blackened fingers, the young man sobbed in compliance and swished from the room, booting Kitty from the doorway as he departed. When he had left, the old woman turned on her husband with renewed fury. "A fine way to greet your son," she snarled. "The boy hasn't been home in five years, and you act like you're not happy to see him. Do you know why I asked Roger to come back? Do you?"

"No. . ."

"I wanted him to see for himself how bad off you are. Now that I have a witness, I can finally have you and that moth-eaten cat put away where you won't be so free with my bird seed. Then I won't have to listen to that blessed vacuum cleaner all day, either. I'm so sick of the racket it makes! When you're gone, I'm going to throw that old thing out in the snow and let it rust--"

As the wife rambled on, Edgar became aware of a sputtering cough coming from behind him. Suddenly, the corner of the room burst into a deafening roar, and the old man was spun around by the cold caress of runaway steel. The din was pierced by a scream, and Edgar whirled around in time to see the wife topple over backward onto the rug with his vacuum cleaner on top of her. As Edgar watched wide-eyed, it worked methodically over her body, humming louder with each pass to hide her shrieks. First, the wife's clothing disappeared into the dust bag. Then one leg. Then

94

another. In a matter of minutes it was over. The wife had simply disappeared. There were no blood stains on the rug. There was no evidence of a struggle. All that remained was Edgar's now silent vacuum sitting in the middle of the room, its unplugged cord dangling idly behind it.

Edgar crossed the carpet and carefully approached his machine. As he drew nearer, he noticed the dust bag, that moments before had bulged obscenely, was now back to its normal size. He might have felt something like relief if it weren't for a sudden tapping that came on the back door.

Stumbling forward, the old mechanic wrapped both arms around his vacuum and cooed to it lovingly until it again started up and began to move across the floor. It positioned itself in the corner of the living room next to the kitchen archway and then shut itself off just as Roger opened the back door. At the same moment, Kitty slithered from beneath the sofa and arched her back against Edgar's leg.

"Mother? Faa-ther?"

Smiling slyly, Edgar peeped around the corner at the son. He could feel Kitty rubbing purringly against him when he said, "Yes, Roger."

"Why didn't you open the door when I knocked a moment ago?"

"I'm sorry. I was busy vacuuming and didn't hear you."

"Well, I had my hands full and couldn't work the knob. I had to set my clothes down on the filthy porch floor, and they got all soiled. Couldn't you or Mother have been more attentive?"

"Bring your clothes in here, Roger," smiled the old man, motioning him into the living room. "We will brush them off for you. We will make all the dirt disappear. . ."

THE EIGHTH WONDER OF THE WORLD

From an overlook built on a rocky hillside, Karl Johnson stared in awe at the Kinzua Viaduct that stretched from ridge top to ridge top 2,053 feet across the valley. The massive structure rose on twenty steel-plated legs from the murky gorge below. In clearer weather he would have seen that the center of the span was over three hundred feet tall. Even obscured by the July rain, to Johnson the viaduct still lived up to its billing as the Eighth Wonder of the World.

Watching the mist swirl about the black bridge, Karl said to his sister who stood shivering beside him, "Hell of a day for Dad's funeral. I guess we better carry out his last request before another downpour drenches us."

"Yeah, it seems weird coming here from such a solemn service," sighed Ruby sadly. "Especially after all the great times we had at this bridge picnicking with Grandma B."

"I just wish I'd been around in 1900 to see our great grandfather help rebuild the viaduct with steel. I always heard he was a fine Swedish craftsman. He also must have known a bit about having kids if you consider Grandma's ten siblings," chuckled Karl.

"How can you joke at a time like this?" snapped Ruby, tears welling in her blue eyes. "You're the one who's going to spread Dad's ashes over the Kinzua Valley."

"Then, let's get to it before I lose my nerve."

Karl left the overlook and led Ruby up a worn trail to the Kinzua Bridge State Park information area. He walked directly to a series of photos encased in glass. He knew the photos traced the history of the viaduct, and he was drawn to them every time he visited. These pictures were like old friends to him.

Karl was still amazed that a group of forty industrious men erected the prefabricated ironwork of the original bridge in just ninety-four days. That was in 1882 when all the workers had to aid them were two steam hoists, a gin pole, and a wooden crane. As he studied the crew's faces, Karl saw the same stubborn persistence that was ingrained in his own character.

"Are you going to stand there gawking all day?" whined Ruby, elbowing her brother in the ribs. "Come on. I'm cold."

"I'll bet you wouldn't be cold if we were looking for the gold buried out here," smiled Karl. "You know how many hours Uncle Dick has spent searching for it."

"Yeah. Yeah. I know all about the bank robber who hid his loot by a triangular rock within sight of the bridge. At least all that snooping Dick did allowed him to spot the rust that's been eating away at the support columns for years. I'm glad he told so many people. Without his lobbying, funds never would have been raised to begin the preservation work. Maybe we shouldn't go out there if Uncle Dick says the bridge is unsafe."

"No, it's alright. The state still hasn't closed it to foot traffic."

"I don't know. . .I'll bet if the repair crew guys weren't rained out today, they'd forbid us to walk over the gorge."

Karl turned up his collar as another squall sent other tourists scurrying for cover. A little rain couldn't drive him away after all the time he spent out in the weather with his dad hunting the whitetail deer that teemed near the bridge. Just up the valley, in the middle of a snowstorm, he had shot his first buck near Grant's Rocks. These rocks had gotten their name when President Ulysses S. Grant came to McKean County to hunt with Kinzua Bridge founder, Thomas Kane, and killed a massive stag there. Although Karl's buck was only a four point, it signaled his passage into manhood and still ranked as one of his favorite memories.

"Karl, there you go daydreaming again," chided Ruby. "It looks like the weather's getting worse. I think we oughta leave."

"You always were the worrier of the Johnson clan," replied her brother. "We'll be okay."

"Even after hearing the severe weather advisory on the radio a thousand times while driving up here? I'm sorry, Karl. I'm going to wait in the car where it's safe."

"Okay, Sis. See you in a little bit."

As Ruby fought her way across the parking lot through the gusty wind, Karl's eyes misted over as he thought back to his many trips to the Kinzua Bridge with his father, Paul. They especially loved to come here to fly balsa wood model airplanes they made from kits bought at Ruth Brother's Hardware in Bradford. It took days to glue together the pieces and cover the wings and bodies with paper. After all that work, they glided their planes from the bridge toward Kushequa, knowing full well they'd never recover them from the thick forest below. The gliders had rubber band powered engines and zoomed with the wind for miles until disappearing from sight. No wonder Dad wanted his ashes scattered over the Kinzua Valley, sighed Karl, as the treasured recollection drifted back into his subconscious.

Karl left the visitors' information area and trudged toward the railroad tracks leading onto the Kinzua Viaduct. As he tramped along, he could hear his Uncle Dick's voice in his head telling how the bridge originally came to be built. "When General Thomas Kane returned from leading his Bucktail Regiment in the Civil War," Dick lectured, "he found his land in McKean County brimming with coal. With Buffalo, New York, using over three million tons of coal a year, Kane needed to find a way to carry his product to market. To accomplish this, he founded the New York, Lake Erie, and Western Railroad and began laying track to the north. To get to Buffalo, he could either take a six mile detour around the Kinzua Valley or build this bridge. Kane decided to span the gorge when he learned how big a pile of greenbacks that would save. The general also wanted to overcome the challenge of building the world's highest bridge. He then contacted the brilliant engineer Octave Chanute, who gave the bid to the Phoenixville Bridge Works. The rest, as they say, is history."

Johnson marched forward cradling his father's burial urn in the crook of his arm. He was unaware of the tears streaming down his face until a fierce wind smacked him as he proceeded onto the bridge walkway. The structure swayed and bucked beneath his feet until he found it increasingly difficult to maintain his balance. With a grim smile Karl remembered the stories of such winds ripping the tops off boxcars and blowing whole cargoes of hemlock bark from the trains. That was why engine speeds were regulated to five miles an hour when they chugged across the trestle.

As Karl inched along holding tightly to the railing, he recalled the time he and his dad were trapped here by a train. When the locomotive rumbled onto the bridge, the swaying of the tracks intensified, causing Paul's face to go pale. Visibly shaken, the elder Johnson straddled a railing post and let his feet dangle off the bridge. He wedged Karl against the post and wrapped his powerful arms around him while the long string of coal cars jarred every bone in their bodies. After the train had rattled past, Paul stood and vomited over the railing. That was the only time the boy had seen his dad frightened. It wasn't until years later that Karl learned how Paul almost fell off the roof of a roundhouse that serviced train engines in Bradford. Since his boyhood in the 1930's, Paul successfully had hid his fear of heights until again faced by sudden danger in a very high place.

Karl fought his way across the bridge until he could see the rain-swollen Kinzua Creek below him through the patchy mist. Gripping the urn more tightly in the crook of his arm, Johnson loosened the lid and said a final prayer for his father's soul. Afterward, he launched Paul's ashes into the wind and watched them blow violently off toward Kushequa.

The wind had now reached gale proportions, and it was all Karl could do to hang onto the railing. Fearfully, he stared out over the valley at the leafy July woods that obscured the rocky terrain. It had been no problem for the builders to quarry sandstone blocks from the neighboring hills, he remembered. These were cut into stone piers and buried thirty-five feet into the ground to anchor the iron legs of the viaduct.

"Too bad the original anchor bolts weren't replaced when the bridge was rebuilt," muttered Karl, feeling the violent sway of the structure beneath him. "That was one of the major concerns that ended excursion train traffic last year."

Johnson dropped to his knees and began crawling toward the park end of the bridge. It took every ounce of strength he could muster to fight the wind assailing him. The sky had turned the color of hard-boiled egg yolks and churned violently. When the wind swirled with tornado intensity, Karl clung desperately to the railing and watched the trees scalped from the hills. It was the last sight he remembered as the railing broke loose, hurling him into the abyss.

Karl extended his arms and legs and floated like a sky diver toward Grant's Rocks. The air was alive with singing shards of metal and splinters of wood. He closed his eyes to keep the wind from plucking them out of their sockets and heard the bridge fight for its life behind him.

Karl glided on the wind's current until he was rocked by a violent collision that sent a sudden numbness through him. Opening his eyes, he found himself immersed in murky light. He felt someone grip his hand. He turned to find his father floating beside him, looking thirty-five again. Paul was dressed in his black and red deer hunting clothes. A broad grin stretched across his face as he pointed toward a glowing tunnel opening through the clouds ahead.

THE DRYWALL MAN

Ruth Jameson paced nervously across her living room carpet wringing her withered hands. "The drywall man said he'd be here an hour ago," she muttered, glancing at the portrait of her deceased husband hanging above the mantle. "These young fellows sure aren't punctual like you were, Reggie dear."

The old lady placed a Glenn Miller record on her phonograph and dropped the needle on the worn, scratchy disc. She danced dreamily, leading an invisible partner, as the music filled the damp room with the warmth of sentimental memories. She waltzed over to a wall completely covered with framed photos that traced her life with her wonderful husband. The same loving smile illuminated Reggie's face in every one of those pictures from their wedding day to their golden anniversary. Oh, how she missed seeing that smile wreathed on his rugged, old mug.

Tearfully, Ruth continued to reminisce until a brash knock resonated up the front hall. Dabbing her eyes with a dainty handkerchief, she turned off the music and scurried to let in her visitor. She swung open the door and found herself face-to-face with a veritable bear of a man. The barrel-chested fellow was squat and thickly built with Gypsy hair curling over his swarthy forehead. He had square, powerful hands and muscular arms from all the mud he had slung. After fixing Ruth with an unflinching stare, he wet his thick lips and said, "Mrs. Jameson, I'm Calvin Scarnati, the drywall man."

"Um. . .Nice to meet you, Mr. Scarnati. Please. Come in."

Calvin squeezed his bulk through the door frame and pushed past the frail woman. "Wow! Look at the structural damage in this hall," he bellowed. "I can see at least twenty cracks coming through that wallpaper. It's gonna cost you big bucks, lady, but I'll have this area in perfect shape before you can say nine hundred dollars."

"Excuse me, but this isn't where I want the work done," replied Ruth, her face flushing with anger and embarrassment. "Why don't you come this way, and I'll show you what I have in mind."

"Okay, but if this was my house, I'd address those cracks ASAP!" blustered Scarnati.

With her hands twitching nervously, Mrs. Jameson led the burly contractor into her living room. "Look up there," she said, pointing to several prominent fissures that transversed the entire length of the ceiling. "Could you fix those for me?"

"No problem, ma'am. Ceilings are my specialty."

"Then how much would you charge for such a job?"

"I'm a $25-an-hour man," said Scarnati proudly. "I've even worked in the mayor's house."

"That's pretty steep," mumbled Ruth, "especially considering that my dear, departed husband did the original work in his spare time for nothing."

"That's your trouble right there. Just by looking at them cracks, I could tell an amateur hung that ceiling."

"Reggie was no amateur, sir!" bristled Mrs. Jameson. "You may have worked for the mayor of this little burg, but my husband remodeled the governor's mansion from top to bottom before we moved here."

"When do you want me to start?" grunted the drywall man, ignoring the old woman's indignation. "I'll need half the money up front."

Ruth gnashed her dentures as she fought to contain her rage. She had phoned every contractor in the Yellow Pages, and this was the only one who even bothered to return her call. Her sons were flying in from the West Coast next month, and she surely didn't want them to see the house in such disrepair. Finally, she said to Scarnati, "And how much will that be?"

"Uh. . .Let's see. Figuring in my time, materials, and transportation cost--"

"Transportation cost?"

"Ain't you seen how expensive gasoline is these days, lady? I gotta charge mileage or go outta business."

"Then how much money will you need?"

"Five hundred bucks should cover it."

"Does that include priming and painting?"

"No, I don't <u>do</u> painting. I have an associate I could call to handle that for you. He only charges $20 an hour."

"Only? No, I'll have my nephew paint the ceiling. He won't charge me anything if I make him a nice lunch. Wait a minute, and I'll write you a check."

"Remember. That's only my down payment."

"I remember alright. . ."

Mrs. Jameson sat knitting in her favorite rocker before the fireplace as she did every evening after dinner. Her needles clicked with agitation while she finished the sleeves of a fancy blue sweater for her grandson. Finally, she turned and addressed her husband's portrait. "Well, Reggie dear," she blustered, "I really did it this time! How could I have been so stupid to give that crook Scarnati five hundred dollars? It's been two weeks since he promised to do the work, and I haven't seen hide nor hair of him since. If he doesn't get here soon--"

Ruth's diatribe was interrupted by a loud, prolonged knock. Glancing out the window, she saw Scarnati's work truck parked in her driveway. The old woman sprang from her seat and bustled down the hall to admit the object of her scorn. She had no sooner swung open the door when the swarthy fellow pushed past her lugging an armload of dusty drop cloths.

"Where are you going with those?" demanded Ruth, grabbing the back of the drywaller's shirt.

"You wanted me to start as soon as possible, so here I am."

"Don't you know it's six o'clock at night? I go to bed at eight."

"I could come back, but, hey, that patch job is gonna take at least three coats of drywall compound to make it blend in. Bein' you're the only customer I got way out here, that's three inconvenient trips to the burbs."

"Then be quick about it," snapped Ruth. "And wipe off those muddy feet before you walk on my carpet."

Ignoring Mrs. Jameson's request, Scarnati tramped into the living room and began spreading his soiled drop cloths over the furniture and the floor. In the process, he got mud and dust everywhere. Then he returned to his truck and brought in pieces of scaffolding that he assembled next to her couch. He swung the side railing wildly about, almost knocking over Mrs. Jameson's most expensive lamp. To keep the old woman from chastising him further, he grunted and growled until he had erected his rolling scaffold.

Next, Calvin lugged in a bucket of drywall goo, a roll of seam tape, and a set of trowel-like knives of various widths. He began slapping the mud on the ceiling, not caring where it splattered below. He worked methodically across the room until he was even with Mr. Jameson's portrait hanging above the mantle. When a big splat of mud flew on the picture, the drywall man's scaffold lurched violently beneath him, almost upending him. "What the hell?" he howled. "Musta forgot to lock the wheels."

Scarnati climbed to the floor and found the brake mechanism still in place. Scratching his head, he went back to work a little more carefully than before. He had the stamina of a bull and never broke a sweat as he worked straight through until 9:00 p.m. to finish the taping and the application of the first coat of mud. As Calvin put away his tools, he bellowed to Mrs. Jameson napping in her rocker, "Hey, lady. Lady? I'll be back tomorrow to sand. Okay?"

Ruth woke with a start and embarrassedly brushed some drool from her chin. Finally, she mumbled, "I guess so, sir. What time shall I expect you?"

"Nine a.m. sharp!"

The drywall man's idea of "sharp" turned out to be noon. Mrs. Jameson fretted as she let him in the door and watched him stomp down the hall ahead of her banging his tool kit against every door jam he squeezed through. Without bothering to drape plastic over the entrance to keep the drywall dust from traveling all over the house, he climbed his scaffolding and began sanding like mad. He had only worked for a few seconds when the sanding sponge flew magically from his hand and landed at the fuming Ruth's feet.

"Dropping that sponge serves you right," the old lady scolded. "How dare you go to work without first sealing off my living room? You get down here right now and get to it."

"Are you telling me how to do my job?" grumbled Scarnati, reluctantly following her instructions.

"Yep! I didn't live with a construction man for fifty years without learning the right way to do things. I didn't see you wearing a mask, either, when you sanded."

"Them's fer sissies," barked Calvin. "I'd just as soon eat dust for dinner as pizza or rigatoni."

Scarnati shooed the old woman out of his way and hung an ample sheet of plastic over the doorway. He even used blue painter's tape to hold it up, so he wouldn't further damage the enamel finish on the woodwork he already banged with his tool kit. Once he was sealed in the room, he sanded his patches with a practiced hand that only came after hundreds of work hours. Then he chose a wider knife to apply a second coat of drywall compound that feathered in his first application. Calvin worked tirelessly for five straight hours to complete his task.

Scarnati emerged from the living room completely covered with white powder. He slapped at his clothes as he stomped down the hall, scattering the dust in his wake. Mrs. Jameson choked and coughed and sputtered until she cleared her throat. Before she could admonish Calvin, he disappeared outside to finish brushing himself off.

"See you tomorrow," the drywall man called through the door he left ajar behind him. Without waiting for a reply, he leaped in his truck and screeched out of the driveway just like he'd been summoned to fight a fire.

Scarnati didn't return the next day or the day after that. Ruth left twelve messages with his answering service before he finally showed up nearly a week later. Without an explanation or apology, he appeared unexpectantly and let himself into the house. The old woman was doing laundry in the basement when she heard his trademark elephant stomp in the room above her. She was so glad he finally came back that she ignored his imprudence and even offered him a Pepsi after emerging from the cellar.

Calvin was too busy to accept Ruth's offer. On and on he sanded until he completed his task three hours later without as much as a restroom break. Come to think of it, reflected the old lady, he hasn't once asked to use the bathroom since he started working for me. He must have a bladder the size of Chicago.

Scarnati was about to leave the living room a second time without dusting off his clothes when a chair skated across the floor to trip him off his feet. He hit the carpet hard, sending a cloud of dust boiling to the ceiling. Choking and swearing, he leaped up to fling open a window. It took many minutes for the dust to settle enough for him to apply his last coat of mud. When Calvin finally finished, he yelled through the plastic draped over the doorway, "Hey, lady, how about tossin' me a damp towel? I wanna clean up before I leave."

"Sure enough, Mister Scarnati. I'll gladly oblige if you'll wipe off your feet, too."

The next day the drywall man actually did show up at the time he promised. He finished his final sanding before lunch and then summoned Mrs. Jameson into the room.

"That's a fine job you did there," said Ruth as she admired Scarnati's flawless work. "I wouldn't even know there'd been any splits in that ceiling."

"Then we need to talk about that other problem you got," bullied Calvin.

"And what problem is that?"

"With them cracks in your hallway."

"But I told you I didn't want to tackle that right now," huffed Ruth.

"First, let me show you something," insisted Scarnati, leading the old woman into the hall. "Look here."

Before Mrs. Jameson could protest, the drywall man whipped a knife from his pocket, snapped open the blade, and began slitting one of the cracks showing through the wallpaper. "Look at how deep this gap is," he thundered. "If this was my house, I'd attend to this directly before there's further deterioration. If you wait much longer, you'll have to replace all the wall board underneath. I'll show you how rotten these walls are."

To emphasize his point, Scarnati slammed his fist right through the wall near the living room archway. His blow hit with such force that many of Ruth's favorite photos jarred from the wall inside. When the old woman heard their frames smash on the floor, she scrambled into the room to find her wedding and honeymoon pictures ruined amid a pile of broken glass.

Suddenly, Ruth heard a surprised grunt, followed by a hoarse yell. She shot into the hall to find Scarnati being ushered rudely across the threshold and out the front door. Unseen hands had him by the scruff of the neck and the seat of his pants, and his feet dragged uselessly behind him. The bum's rush he received was so violent that he flew halfway across the yard before falling heavily on his face. When his hat sailed out the door after him, the drywall man scrambled for his truck without fetching his equipment or collecting the rest of the money owed him.

"Thank you, dear," said Mrs. Jameson, shuffling into the living room to address the portrait of her late husband. "I wondered how far you'd let that crooked man push me. Now, I know you still love me. Just as much as I love you, Reggie dear. . ."

AN EMPTY CHAIR

An empty chair sat facing
an untenanted mirror.
Threadbare it sagged
from the weight of dying.
Springs erupted
from broken cushions
& the arms were split
like weatherbeaten lips.
Although it was
bowed & broken,
ghosts still savored
its musty perfume.

ESTRANGED

Charlie Watson emerged from a heavy sleep. A faint buzz, he recognized as a rattler's warning, pricked his senses and brought his brain to full alert. Cautiously, he opened his eyes as sweat popped on his brow and his pulse pounded with fear. Glancing warily about, he searched for the fang-bared reptile that must have crawled through the torn screen door of his Florida bungalow. He moved his hand an inch at a time until it touched the handle of the nightstand drawer where he stashed his pistol. It wasn't until he had eked the drawer half open that he realized the saurian buzzing came from his telephone.

With a shiver, Watson snatched up the receiver and grunted, "Hello?"

"Is that you, Charlie?"

"I'm the only one living here. Of all people, you should know that, Lauren."

"Just because we're separated, you don't have to be nasty," replied a silky voice.

"What do ya want?"

"Well, I'm down at the airport and need a lift to your mother's house. I didn't think it would be proper if I stayed with you. . .until we patch up our differences."

"At my mother's?" gasped Charlie. "Does she know you're coming?"

"Of course, silly. I called her from Chicago last week."

"And she agreed to let you in her house?"

"She still loves me, Charlie. Even if you don't. Why, you make me sound like some kind of monster."

"Aren't you?"

"Won't you come pick me up? P-P-Please?"

"But I just pulled a double shift at the knife factory, Lauren. Why can't you take a cab?"

"Same old Charlie. Gone from an alcoholic to a workaholic just like that! If you ever cared for me even a little, you gotta come down. I-I-I-I don't have money for a taxi."

"Alright! Give me an hour. What time is it, anyway?"

"Noon."

Watson slammed down the receiver, crawled groggily to his feet, and pulled on a rumpled pair of work pants. After slugging down two cups of coffee, he washed his face and ran a comb through his thick, iron-colored hair. He hardly recognized the wrecked visage that stared back at him from the mirror. Five years of ceaseless toil had eroded deep creases in his forehead and turned his eyes into listless pools of sludge. Even his Sundays were no fun. That was when he did his laundry, cleaned his house, and helped his widowed mother with her bills and chores.

"It's like I've been working on a chain gang since Lauren and I became estranged," muttered Charlie. "I'd like to move. Start over again. But then what would poor Mother do? She's such a kind person, she'd see the good in Jeffrey Dahmer! My shrink would call her an 'enabler.' I just wish Mom would see Lauren for the conniving bitch she is."

Charlie banged shut the door behind him but didn't bother to lock it. Except for the pistol, he knew there was nothing worth stealing in the whole house. He had no television or stereo. His furniture was all secondhand. His refrigerator leaked Freon. The stove had a sprung oven door.

"Why in the hell did Lauren have to come back?" puzzled Watson. "She kills everything she touches, man. Every nerve, every heart, every soul! Now, she's gonna screw up my only working relationship--the one with my mother."

Charlie crawled behind the wheel of his VW Bug and bounced down the one-lane dirt track through the Glades he now called home. Twice he had to stop and let gators slither off the road. Exotic birds, plumed in bright blues and greens, squawked at his intrusion, while rabbits fled into the brush on every straightaway. Haunted by scary flashbacks of his marriage to Lauren, he finally arrived at the highway after four bumpy miles.

Charlie's alertness increased as the traffic grew heavier with each mile he sped toward Miami. Soon, he was weaving in and out of a constant flow of passenger cars, SUVs, and oversized tractor trailers. After swearing at an obnoxious trucker that swerved in front of him each time he tried to pass, he glanced fuming out the window at the squat, stucco dwellings lining the Tamiami Trail.

"Look at the bars on those windows," he grunted. "And that's in the houses. I may be imprisoned by my work, but at least I don't _live_ in jail."

Watson cut off a honking tourist and veered into the Miami International Airport. He hated the bustle of the place and the deafening roar of airliners as they took off or landed. After screeching into a parking spot, he locked his car and shifted his wallet to his front pocket. He was carrying a week's salary for his mortgage payment and didn't need to be mugged by the Cuban greasers that frequented the corridors and restrooms. Somehow the lock blade knife he always carried in his pocket didn't seem enough protection here, even though it was daytime. To be doubly safe, he pissed behind a Dodge Caravan before entering the air-conditioned terminal.

Near the service desk stood a willowy redhead dressed in a tasteful blue skirt and dark blue stockings. Her hair was tied into a bun favored by the professional women of South Florida. She puffed casually on a cigarette that protruded from rich, vermilion lips. She had an actress' cheekbones and nose, and would have been described as beautiful, if not for the age lines that even a heavy coat of makeup couldn't hide. When she spotted Charlie pushing through the crowd, she waved and rushed to give him a stiff hug.

"I-I-I thought you weren't coming," said Lauren with a hurt whimper. "I told your mother we'd be arriving around two. It's almost two-thirty now! You know how much Clara values punctuality."

"It's not that far to Hallandale," reminded Charlie gruffly. "We'll be there soon enough without your nagging."

"I'm only thinking of your mother. At least she'll be happy to see me."

"And it looks like you're planning to stay with her quite a while," Watson grunted as he struggled with two oversized suitcases. "You'll have to carry the smaller bags yourself."

Charlie broke trail through a jostling crowd surging for the exits. Using one of his wife's suitcases, he smacked open a terminal door and led her on through the congested parking lot. Twice he had to set down his burdens to ease the quivering of his muscles. Twice more she begged him to stop, so she could rest.

"At least no one swiped my tires this time," puffed Watson upon spotting his Volkswagen Beetle.

"That's right!" recalled Lauren. "Someone stripped our BMG the last time you picked me up here. That's when I was a buyer for Jordache, and you were a power broker. I thought you were going to blow a fuse!"

"You mean like I did when seeing you now!" snapped Charlie, slamming his wife's luggage into the trunk. "We'll squeeze the rest of your bags in the backseat. It looks like the mothers will fit!"

Watson scrambled behind the wheel and reached over to unlock the passenger side door. His wife had barely seated herself when he floored it. Before she could snap on her seat belt, he squealed for the lot gate and shot into the street. After nearly sideswiping a convertible blaring rap music, he blasted up the on ramp to I-90. When his VW joined the normal ebb and flow of the northbound traffic, Lauren finally squeaked, "How long have you been Speed

Racer?"

"Since I quit drinking, and my reflexes returned. I drive like this to survive on roads jammed with crazy fools."

"Do you isolate yourself in the swamp to survive, too?"

"Yeah, just like you became hell on high heels!"

"What happened to us, anyway, Charlie?" asked Lauren, reaching to stroke her husband's arm.

"What didn't happen would be a better question," replied Watson, stiffening. "All those lavish parties and trips to Key West we couldn't afford and the half-dozen maxed-out credit cards. Yes, and we can't forget the drinking. And the way you wrapped yourself like a snake around any fellow who looked at you in Key West and at those lavish parties. Jealousy is like poison, in case you've forgotten."

"But how about the good times?"

"In bed?"

"Yeah, you know--"

"You mean I learned!" growled Charlie, pushing away his wife's groping hand. "Wasn't there a song about using sex as a weapon? I don't know why you came back here, but I won't be included in your games."

The ride to Hallandale was a silent one after Charlie's outburst. Watson kept his eyes peeled on the highway as he wove in and out of traffic with precise spurts of speed. Lauren, meanwhile, stared out the window at the distant beach. Her face was perfectly serene as if she were riding with a beloved husband who always obeyed the speed limit.

Finally, the VW swerved into the right lane and swooped onto a street heading due east. The car hadn't gone more than a couple blocks before it wheeled left up a circular drive and screeched to a stop before a tile-roofed house set in the midst of a manicured lawn. The front door flew open and out rushed a fragile, elderly woman dressed in dirty-kneed khaki pants and a straw hat. Lauren exploded from the VW to greet her, and the two hugged like long-lost sisters.

"Well, Mother, it looks like you and Lauren have a

lot of catching up to do," muttered Charlie, dumping his estranged wife's luggage on the front stoop. "I guess I better be shoving off."

"Aren't you at least going to stay long enough to cart in dear Lauren's things?" chided Clara Watson, wagging a bony finger at her son.

"Sorry, Mom. My shift starts at the plant in a half-hour, so I really need to get going. I see you're in your work clothes. Can't you help her?"

"Well, at least now I won't have to depend on you to drive me around!" snapped Clara. "Lauren will have full use of the family Oldsmobile."

"You should have learned to drive yourself after Dad died. Then you wouldn't need to rely on anyone."

"And become a hermit like you, son? Show some respect! Will I be seeing you Sunday?"

"Yeah, the Sunday Lauren leaves," replied Charlie, giving his mom a quick hug. "I think it's best I stay away, knowing how my arguing with Lauren always upsets you. Call me if you need anything."

Charlie floated in a very dark place where the sky and ocean were the exact same temperature and hue. Rollers crashed on a distant beach, and the haunted shriek of gulls echoed from a fog bank. The fin of a great shark cut the water just behind him and immediately submerged. Charlie began swimming for all he was worth. No matter how fast his legs kicked, he could feel an evil presence closing on him. He thrashed his arms and dug his hands in the churning sea until a shadow shot past him. He fought through a turbulence of bubbles and discovered the predator loomed directly in his path. It was long and sleek and deadly with a slashing, triangular tail. A mouth full of razor teeth glittered in its bullet head. With a menacing swirl, it dove at him. Closer and closer it charged until Watson found himself staring into the cold, glittery, unmistakable eyes of Lauren.

Charlie screamed and sat straight up in bed. In his ears echoed a sharp bleat that he eventually recognized as the telephone. The sound stalled after ten rings and then started over again. It wasn't until the third sequence of rings that the trembling man grabbed the receiver and croaked, "Hello?"

"Charlie! This is your mother," squawked a frightened voice. "You need to come over here right away!"

"Over where?"

"To my house. Where else?"

"What's wrong?"

"It's Lauren. Her pulse is irregular. She's hyperventilating. And falling all over the place--"

"Like a drunk?"

"W-W-Well, yes. And I can't. . .control her. I'm afraid she'll hurt herself."

"Why don't you call 911?"

"Oh, Charlie! What would the neighbors think? You come quick! You hear?"

There was a click on the line followed by a droning dial tone. Still shaking from his dream, Charlie raced out to his car and screeched off through the night. When he arrived in Hallandale and whipped up his mother's drive, every window of her house was ablaze with light. Not bothering to knock, he bolted inside and found his mother bawling on the living room sofa. Just then, Lauren staggered up the hall dressed in a provocative nighty. With glittering eyes, she leered at him and then fell flat on her face.

Charlie dragged his wife roughly to her feet. She clung to him, cooing madly, pressing her half-bared breasts against him. Then, she produced some matches and a pack of Kools from her bosom. She lit a cigarette and tossed the still burning match on the rug. As Watson leaped to stomp it out with his work boots, Lauren cackled and fell hard on her backside. She smacked against a table, upending a treasured family vase full of fresh-cut flowers. Before Clara could grab it, the vase toppled to the floor to shatter into a thousand knife-like shards. Lauren laughed again and rose to totter through the destruction, cutting her bare feet to ribbons. Before she could do any more damage to herself or the house, Charlie swept her into his arms and whisked her out to the VW. His mother, toting Lauren's bathrobe, loped behind them and crawled blubbering into the backseat.

"What's wrong with her?" cried Mrs. Watson, placing the bathrobe around her daughter-in-law's shoulders. "We've gotten along so well this past month. . .Until tonight."

"She fell off the wagon, Mother. Can't you see? I-I-I used to act like this, too. Until I quit boozing. Watching Lauren's antics cured me. If only she could see how she acts. When toasted."

"But I didn't smell anything on her breath. And she's been going to AA meetings faithfully every night. Why, the day she arrived, she told me all about her battles with alcohol."

"Vodka doesn't have an odor. I've watched this drama a thousand times, Mother. I'm surprised she hasn't gone on Jerry Springer and performed her act for the whole damn country."

"But Lauren's been the perfect guest. She cleans the house, helps me in the garden, makes out my bills, does my banking--"

"Banking?"

"Why, yes. She even had the forethought of having my money put in both your names in case something should happen to me."

"Both our names?"

"You are still married aren't you? And she's always been like a sweet daughter from the time she came into this family. For the life of me, I can't understand why you don't work out your differences with the dear girl. I'll bet Lauren's acting this way because she loves you and wants to get your attention."

Gritting his teeth, Charlie turned into the hospital and stopped at the emergency room door. He threw Lauren over his shoulder, stomped into the waiting room, and deposited her into a padded chair. As his mother spoke with the nurse and attended to the paperwork, he returned outside to park

118

his VW. Then he walked across the street to a sports bar where he ordered a hamburger and a Coke. "It's gonna be hours before they attend to Lauren," he muttered. "Might as well feed my face in the meantime. I'd have a real drink, but who knows where that would lead?"

Charlie plopped on a bar stool and buried his head in his hands. He was already stressed to the breaking point from all the double shifts he was working and didn't need this added hassle. Since his company's business doubled after 9/11, he was ceaselessly bent over his grinding wheel putting the edge on military knife blades. Engrossed in his highly dangerous work, he never spoke to anyone or took more than the manditory lunch break. Twice he had had near fatal accidents when knives had slipped from his cramped fingers and had whipped out the top of his machine just past his head. Chewing on his tasteless burger, he almost wished they'd hit him and ended the disaster of his life.

As dawn crept into the sports bar window, Charlie rose from his stool, strode to a pay phone, and wrangled with his employer until he got the day off. Afterward, he crossed the street to find his mother sitting alone behind the drawn curtains of a room on the first floor. "Where's Lauren?" he grumbled. "Off for tests, I suppose."

"No, she ducked out the side door--to smoke."

"Smoke?"

"Yeah, even after the nurse told her ten times to stay put. Why can't she be good?"

Before Charlie could answer, an attendant dressed in green scrubs led the limping Lauren into the room. "You have to sit, ma'am," he commanded, obviously annoyed.

"Whatever. . ." slurred Charlie's wife, flopping on the bed to expose her naked buttocks through the slit in her hospital gown. "Thanks, you big, strong man."

Flushing, the attendant hurried from the room. As soon as he was gone, Lauren popped up and again headed for the exit. This time, Watson leaped to block her path and wrestle her onto the bed.

119

"Stop it, you two!" cried Clara, bursting into tears. "Your behavior is giving our family a black eye! I see these nurses at the market all the time. And at the bank and flower shop. Stop it, I say!"

"Stop what?" bellowed a bossy-looking RN bursting through the curtain. "Is the Mrs. misbehaving again? Lucky for her, her blood work is back from the lab. You can take her home now."

"But what made her act so...crazy?" blubbered Clara.

"Nothing that a pot of black coffee can't cure."

"Or a good shrink," added Charlie sourly. "Get dressed, Lauren. We'll be waiting out in the hall."

Moments later, Lauren stumbled through the curtain, pulling her nighty over her head. She flashed two male attendants wheeling a gurney onto an elevator and then snatched the car keys from her angry husband's hand. "I'm--gonna--drive--home," she sang in a little girl's voice. "I'm--gonna--drive--home."

Lauren shot through the emergency room and dashed into the half vacant parking lot, oblivious to her heavily bandaged feet. She sprinted for the VW Bug and ripped open the door. Charlie caught up to her just as she stuck the key into the ignition and fired up the engine. Leaving a deep bruise on her arm, Watson restrained her before she could reach for the gear shift.

"You're mean!" Lauren whined, slapping at her husband with a flurry of limp-wristed blows.

"And you're screwed in the head!"

"But I can drive your mommy's car anytime I want," she taunted. "Anytime I want!"

A drowning woman's voice gurgled through Charlie's consciousness. It rose like bubbles from the depths of the sea, fighting through his need for sleep. The louder it gurgled, the more familiar it became. Over and over it cried his name until he broke through the surface of reality where the voice morphed into the nonstop ringing of his telephone.

"Yes," he croaked into the receiver. "What is it?"

120

"I'm sorry to disturb you at such a late hour, sir," intoned a rote voice, "but there's been an accident."

"Accident?"

"Involving your mother and wife."

"Car accident?"

"Yes."

"How are they?"

"It might be better if you come to the North Miami Hospital and see for yourself. Do you know where we're located, sir? Sir?"

Charlie slammed down the phone and then rooted in his nightstand drawer for his pistol. "With all those Cubans prowling about, it's not safe in that damn city after dark," he grunted, pulling the Smith & Wesson .38 from beneath a pile of rumpled handkerchiefs. "Where's my protection permit? I'll need that for sure."

Stashing his gun in his coat pocket, Charlie shot out the door and scrambled behind the wheel of his Beetle. He spun off down the road through a torrential downpour, nearly hitting the doe and two fawns that often visited him from the swamp. A possum and her litter weren't so lucky. He barely felt their thump beneath his wheels before blasting through an endless series of puddles toward the blacktop highway.

The trip to the hospital was a blur. What Charlie found inside was a nightmare. His mother lay in intensive care with her broken legs elevated and tubes running up her nose. As shadows played across her deeply bruised face, a bleeping monitor traced her battle with death. He stayed until the life ebbed out of her, and the bleeps were replaced by an awful silence.

Charlie had not thought of his estranged wife until the rushing tread of rubber soles echoed up the corridor. Empty, he rose and staggered to the nurse's station. There, he mumbled to a woman in flowered togs, "Where can I find my wife, Lauren Watson? Is she in intensive care, too?"

"No, she didn't need much treatment. Let me see. She's in Room 425. You'll be pleased to know she only got a few cracked ribs from the horrible collision on Route One that's been all over the news. That should ease your sorrow over losing your mother. I just heard. I'm so sorry. . ."

"Yeah, right!"

Charlie wheeled and stormed past the busy elevator. Flying down a flight of stairs, he slammed open the fourth floor door and stalked angrily up the hall. After knocking the bedpans from a candy striper's cart, he mowed down a doctor backing from a scrub room. He saw nothing and knew nothing but the gnawing need for revenge.

When Watson stomped into Room 425, he found his wife smoking in bed. As he strode toward her, she flashed him a bright smile and giggled, "Why, Charlie, you're the one who looks like he's been in an accident. Aren't you glad I'm okay?"

"You killed Mother!" he growled. "Don't you know that?"

"I suspected as much after watching the paramedics work on her."

"You cold-blooded bitch!"

"Oh, lighten up, husband," advised Lauren. "After we inherit all that money Clara had stashed away, you won't have to work so hard ever again."

"So that's why you came back?"

"And to love you."

"Plunge me back into hell, you mean!" snarled Watson, snatching up a pillow.

"What are you going to do, smother me? You don't have the balls, dear," said Lauren, flicking her cigarette ash at Charlie.

"Don't I?"

"No, all you know how to do is run away. From your feelings. From me."

"But from Mom's murder?"

"No one will believe the wreck wasn't an accident, Daddy," smiled Lauren, slipping into her little girl's voice. "I skid on the wet road is all. And hit a semi. Too bad Clara's seat belt didn't catch. Now, forget all that bad talk. Give me a nice, big hug--"

Charlie yanked the pistol from his coat pocket. He

had meant to use the pillow to deaden the muzzle blast, so he could get away--clean. His eyes were so clouded with anger, he forgot to line up his sights. He jerked the trigger six times, and all six shots went astray.

Lauren, meanwhile, sat coolly dragging on her cigarette. By the way Charlie's pistol wobbled, she knew she had nothing to fear. When her husband's gun clicked empty, she taunted, "Missed as usual, didn't you, dear?"

Watson's face went suddenly pale, and he moaned in utter futility. He began shaking uncontrollably as his last shred of manhood slipped away. When a flood of tears blinded him, he let the pistol clatter to the floor.

"Poor, poor Charlie," cooed Lauren, rising to snare him in her embrace. She ran her fingers through his sweat-sodden hair. She stroked his streaming cheeks. She wrapped herself around him like a snake.

When security finally burst into the room, they found Charlie Watson lying comatose on the bed. Lauren was bent prayerfully over him, weeping like she hadn't just inherited nine hundred grand. "My husband's had a major breakdown," she sobbed. "Help him. Please! Please, please help dear Charlie."

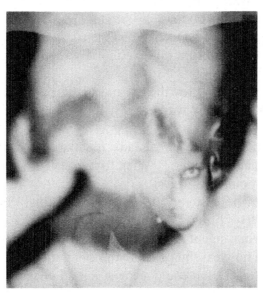

BAD THINGS HAPPEN TO BAD MEN

"Where's Ellen's alimony check?" snarled the lawyer's voice in Dylan March's ear. "She's had it with your procrastination crap."

"And I'm sick of her bitchery," muttered Dylan into the phone. "Isn't a divorce supposed to end a couple's misery? In every religion I've heard of, there's life after death."

"Always a wise guy, aren't you, pal?"

"Yeah, even with a hangover," replied March, grabbing his throbbing forehead.

"Well, wise guy, this is what's going down. You will either have Ellen's check by Friday, or my associates will confiscate your photography equipment for me. What they'll do for their own pleasure is another matter."

"You can't do that!"

"Bad things happen to bad men."

"But that'd ruin my livelihood. Then how will I pay anything?"

"By finally growing up and getting a real job. As I see it, that's the only way Ellen will ever get what's coming to her."

"The bloodsucker already has the house, the camp, and the bank account. What more can she want, the proverbial pound of flesh?"

"I'm not listening to any more of this!" barked the lawyer. "By Friday! Understand? After a little arm twisting, your agent gladly told me how to locate you. There'll be no weaseling out of your obligation this time."

Before Dylan could answer, a loud click reverberated

in his head. He let his cell phone slip from his fingers and fall on the worn rug. Exhaling a low sigh, he flopped back into bed to watch the sun set behind the neon GET_YS_URG MOT_L sign. He had somehow lost a whole day, and he knew his bacon really was fried this time.

"Shouldn't have stayed out 'til beer-thirty chasin' skirts," March groaned. "Hell, I missed the big cavalry reenactment I was sent here to photograph for <u>Blue and Gray Magazine</u>. Fat chance the 'zine will pay my expenses now. And what about the grand I own Bitchzilla? I better come up with some way to make a few thou or blow this dive quick!"

Dylan rolled over and covered his head with a lumpy pillow. His temples pounded with the effort, and his stomach churned mightily. He hadn't laid still for more than a minute when he knew he would be sick. Staggering into the bathroom, he bent over the toilet just in time to retch and gag horribly. A bout of the dry heaves followed until he was too spent to worry about anything other than returning to bed. In the end it was easier to collapse on the floor. He hardly felt the coldness of the tile when he crumpled up near the sink.

The next thing Dylan remembered was an urgent poking and the breathy whispers of "You alright, mister? Mister? Mister?"

The photographer's eyes popped open to find a frightened maid bent over him. He almost laughed aloud when he saw her garish orange apron and yellow rubber gloves. Her hair reminded him of cat's fur. It stuck out every which way from beneath her polka dot kerchief.

"My sugar's actin' up again," lied March, crawling groggily to his feet. "That's why I passed out. What time is it, anyhow?"

"Time for you to quit boozin'," replied the maid, fanning her hand in front of her nose.

"No, really. What time is it?"

"Ten a.m. Checkout's in an hour."

"Not for me. I have reservations 'til Saturday. What are you doin' in here, anyway? I didn't think you cleaned occupied rooms."

"I do when they turn into pigstys."

"Start out in the bedroom then, will ya? 'Til I get spruced up."

"You could start by brushing them teeth," replied the maid, again waving her hand in front of her nose.

Dylan shooed the protesting woman out of the bathroom and slammed the door behind her. *I wonder which one of the Lee sisters she is?* he thought. *Ug Lee or Home Lee?*

"You better hurry up in there," yelled the maid through the door. "I got work to do!"

"Yeah! Yeah!"

Bending over the sink, the photographer splashed some cold water on his face and then ran a comb through his wavy, blonde hair. *I still got it,* he grinned, examining his boyish features in the mirror. *Not a barfly alive would suspect I was pushin' the far side of forty. Who needs Viagra when he flows like Niagara?*

Just to aggravate the maid, March took his time shaving. He could hear her in the next room muttering to herself as she changed the sheets on the bed. After slapping on a healthy dose of aftershave, he swaggered out of the bathroom and shouted to the woman, "It's all yours, mama. Knock yourself out."

Dylan strutted into the motel lounge and fed two quarters and a dime into the Coke machine. "Ah-h-h," he smirked after popping open the can. "The breakfast of derelicts." Then the photographer plopped into a soft recliner and snatched The Gettysburg Times from a coffee table. Ignoring the grim news from Iraq splashed across the front page, he turned directly to the entertainment section. After checking out which bands were playing at the local bars, he strayed across the headline, "Reenactors Needed for Video Shoot."

With excitement gleaming in his eyes, Dylan read aloud: "Attention, Civil War reenactors. American Talent's latest winner, Sherry Silver, will be in Gettysburg on Friday,

July 10th, to shoot her first music video. Union soldiers are needed as extras for this event. Extras will be chosen from 4-6 p.m. Thursday, July 9th, at the Gettysburg Wax Museum. Uniform authenticity is a must."

"Hot damn!" whistled Dylan. "How much would Star Magazine pay for professional photos of that shoot? I'll get right on it."

Dylan scrambled out the door and bolted down Steinwehr Avenue to the sutler's shop he remembered was only a block away. When he arrived, he found the placed packed with a rabid mob of jostling customers. With all the good clothes long gone, fat men tried to squeeze into small Union jackets, tall fellows struggled with highwater trousers, and scrawny guys rifled the kid's section. When the photographer reached to grab the last blue sack coat dangling on a long, empty rack, a desperate wannabe reenactor pushed him aside and snarled, "That's mine!"

"What do you mean, yours?" yelped March, grabbing the left sleeve. "Gimme it!"

The two men played tug-of-war with the disputed coat, nearly ripping it in half. They pushed and yanked and yanked and cursed until a clerk burst from behind the cash register like a perturbed hen. "Shame on you two," she clucked, slapping at the combatants with a long broom. "Ever since the American Talent people came to town, everyone's gone mad."

Dylan ducked to escape a blow aimed at his head. At the same instant, the coat slipped out of his grasp. His rival went flying into a group of customers gathered at the belt counter. This caused another ruckus, and the beleaguered clerk charged off leveling her broom like a musket.

Still sweating from his skirmish, Dylan circled the shop to search for the other gear he would need to portray a Union soldier. He soon discovered that no blue kepis remained on the hat racks and that just gray canteens dangled from pegs near the cash register. The only brogans remaining were size six, and they were marked up to double the normal price.

The photographer cursed in frustration. He was about to leave the madhouse when he noticed a rack of white dusters jammed in a corner. Above them hung a wide assortment of straw hats. A smile flickered across his face when he saw the dusters. Nonchalantly, he crossed the room and began trying them on until he found one that fit. As luck would have it, the first straw hat he grabbed was just his size.

"Oh, so now you're goin' for a buggy ride?" jeered the fellow he had fought for the sack coat.

"Sure," lied Dylan. "Anything's better than hasslin' with you maniacs."

The photographer pushed his way to the cash register and breathed a sigh of relief when his purchases cleared on his nearly maxed-out credit card. Hustling through the door, he ran down the street to a hardware store. There he purchased a saw, a brush, four 2x2's, plywood, wood glue, and a quart of brown latex paint. These items also were under his credit limit, so he returned to the motel with his arms full and his head swimming with happy plans.

At three-thirty that afternoon Dylan climbed in his rented Olds and roared off to the Wax Museum. By the time he arrived, the parking lot was jammed with reenactors who strutted about showing off their authentic gear. There were Zouaves in baggy red pants, an assortment of blue-coated infantry, and even a few Bucktail skirmishers with Sharps rifles slung over their shoulders. The most awesome of all, though, was the troop of Yankee cavalry. Dressed like the gaudy General Custer's men, they came clattering up the street on their mounts waving their sabers and howling out "Charge!" Their dramatics were wasted because the American Talent director, Mr. Frank, didn't arrive in his silver Mercedes until after the cavalry had cantered into the lot and dismounted.

As soon as Dylan spotted the director, he leaped out of his car and pulled an old-fashioned camera mounted on a tripod from the backseat. Using the tripod as a weapon, he fought his way through the mob to the registration table. By then, the director had chosen some Iron Brigade reenactors and Custer's cavalry for the shoot.

"Who might you be portraying?" asked Mr. Frank when he spied March in his long, white duster and straw hat.

"Alexander Gardner. He was the photographer who shot many famous photos of the Gettysburg Battle. No Civil War video would be complete without a member of the 1860's news media present."

"But we don't allow cameras on the location," Frank said.

"This isn't a real camera," assured Dylan. "Although it's an exact replica of the one that took tintype photos, it isn't functional. I should know. I built it this morning."

"Okay. You're hired. I'll need your name for the payroll."

"I'm Dylan March. Where and when do I report, sir?"

"The video shoot's at the Devil's Den. It will begin promptly at ten a.m. Be there an hour early."

"Why, isn't that appropriate," Dylan beamed.

"What do you mean?" asked the director.

"Alexander Gardner's most famous photo was of a Rebel sharpshooter at that very location. See you at nine o'clock."

"Here's your pass, March. You'll need it to get through security."

"Thanks!"

Suppressing his glee, the photographer went directly back to the motel and had a quiet dinner in the lounge. Instead of the usual Tom Collins, he ordered a tall glass of ice tea with his rare steak. He chewed his food mechanically when it came. To calm his nerves, he looked out the window until the motel sign glowed to life at dusk.

With a smirk, Dylan dropped ten pennies and a worthless poker chip on the table for the waitress. Then he strode back to his room and picked up the camera he had built. Screwing off the top, he installed his new Nikon inside, so that it would shoot through the front shutter of his replica. The Nikon was a state-of-the-art voice activated model that didn't require any button pushing to operate it.

"Now, I can take all the pics of hot Sherry Silver that I want," gloated March when he finished concealing his modern camera. "No one will suspect a thing."

Grinning craftily, Dylan returned to the lounge to learn the exact time. Afterward, he set his alarm clock and checked it twice before crawling in bed at ten o'clock. Only then did his excitement overspill, and he spent half the night tossing and turning on the mattress. Winding himself in and out of his sheets, he kept muttering, "Got to get some shuteye. Big day tomorrow. Big day. Can't screw up again. Not again. . ."

March's eyes popped open at the first squawk of the alarm. Springing out of bed, he scrambled into his reenactor's garb and charged into the bathroom to paste on a phony moustache and some sideburns. He also blackened his eyebrows to make them more prominent. As he slicked down his shock of blonde hair, he chortled, "Gotta make myself pretty for Sherry Silver. Who knows? Maybe I'll get to charm her between takes."

Dylan snatched up his camera and ran out the door to his rental car. It took many turns of the key to fire up the Olds, and he cursed impatiently under his breath until the engine finally rolled over.

The photographer sped south through the sleepy village of Gettysburg and on down the length of Cemetery Ridge. He was too busy counting the dollars he was going to make to heed the many monuments and cannons he passed along the way. He veered right into a shallow valley and then squealed left onto Crawford Avenue. He hadn't gone far before he encountered a roadblock set up by the American Talent security staff. March slowed to a stop, showed his pass to a tough looking guard, and then drove through to a jumble of rocks spilling down the hill to his right.

"Boy, they didn't name this place the Devil's Den for nothing," whistled Dylan. "From the brochure I read, these rocks were a gathering place for huge, poisonous snakes.

Locals claim that Indians held weird ceremonies here, too. Add the ghosts of the Yanks and Rebs killed during the battle, and I sure wouldn't want to be out here at night."

Another security guard directed Dylan into a parking space at the foot of the Devil's Den. Jumping out of his car, the photographer grabbed his camera and followed a company of Yankee reenactors around to the back of the labyrinth of rocks. There he found a long stage built between two boulders. The American Talent logo was anchored at the back and obscured much of the rock wall behind it. Stacks of amplifiers rose on each end of the stage, while band equipment dominated the center. The musicians had just arrived and began an impromptu sound check to make sure their instruments were in tune and that the monitors were positioned correctly.

Dylan continued to gawk at the many preparations going on around him when Director Frank grabbed him by the arm and said, "March, I want you to stand directly in front of the stage and pretend to shoot photos of the action. I've hired two other gents to portray Civil War reporters. They'll stand next to you and scribble notes when the video camera pans this way. That was a great idea you had to include the old-time media."

"Thank you," replied March, grinning broadly. "How are you going to involve the other reenactors?"

"The infantry will be hiding in the rocks, firing their weapons. The cavalry will make a dramatic charge at the end, but that will be shot later today at another part of the battlefield. Why, look! Miss Silver has arrived. I better go and make sure she understands her part in the action."

The director bustled onto the stage just as an attractive, buxom blonde made her entrance. She was dressed in a long Civil War period dress and had her hair tucked beneath a crocheted snood. Wearing less eyeliner, she could have stepped right out of 1863.

Mr. Frank held a quick conference with Sherry and her band. Afterward, he positioned the Union infantry among the boulders and behind a stone wall. By then, two reenactors dressed in old-fashioned suits and derbies had joined Dylan in front of the stage. As the journalists fetched note pads and pencils from their pockets, the photographer scrambled to set up his camera directly in front of Miss Silver.

When the director returned to center stage, Dylan shouted up to him, "Excuse me, sir. Shouldn't those be Rebel snipers over there among the rocks? According to history, the Confederates held this position."

"Our video is for the teen market," replied Frank smugly. "What do kids care about history?"

The director had no sooner spoken when he appeared to trip over his own feet. Stumbling dangerously across the stage, he crashed into a stack of amplifiers before righting himself.

"Who pushed me?" Frank bellowed, whirling around to confront Sherry's bass player.

"Not me, man," squeaked the musician, flushing with embarrassment.

"Well, somebody did! Get ready. We're about to roll."

The director motioned with his hand, and three video cameras were pushed in on dollies to cover all angles of the set. Another camera was focused on the Union soldiers hiding about the Devil's Den. When all were in position, the director shouted, "Quiet! Take One! Action!"

On cue, Sherry Silver stepped up to the microphone stand and bowed her head over it. Her band, meanwhile, began a somber introduction complete with a funeral drumroll. This went on for a full thirty seconds as the vocalist prayed for a lover killed in combat. Blinking back real tears, she murmured in conclusion, "But I won't mourn. I can't mourn. Remembering the heat of your embrace."

After Silver finished her spiel, the musicians blasted into a furious rock assault complete with screeching guitar. While the drummer pummeled his kit like a man possessed, the bassist thumped on his instrument until the Devil's Den shook with the flailing beat. As the music reached it crescendo, Sherry let out a licentious wail and ripped off her prim dress. Beneath was a skintight velvet, blue bikini that caused Dylan to drool so much he almost forgot to order his camera to snap photos.

The vocalist screamed and moaned as much as she sang while shimmying through an oversexed devil dance. She only made it a short way into the song before the bass amp exploded with a thunderous crack, filling the stage with a cloud of noxious smoke.

"Cut! Cut!" yelled the director. "Get a fire extinguisher. Quick!"

The explosion sent the band scurrying for the wings. Sherry screamed at the top of her lungs until Dylan rushed forward, leaped onto the stage, and led her to safety. "Calm down, darlin'," he pleaded, stroking her bare shoulders. "Calm down before you strain those precious vocal chords."

"Get away from me, you creep!" screeched the singer when she felt Dylan's hand fondling her bosom.

"But Sherry, b-b-baby!" cooed Dylan. "Is that a way to treat your hero?"

"Zero is more like it! Security! Escort this creep back into the pit where he belongs."

With feigned indignity, March leaped off the stage before the guards reached him. Returning to his camera, he took a few shots of the bedlam caused by the explosion. It took a half-hour to extinguish the fire, calm everyone's nerves, and replace the damaged equipment. Sherry also had to be redressed and reassured. By the time order was restored, the sun had risen to where it shone directly on the stage, causing too much glare for the shoot to continue.

With a frustrated growl, Mr. Frank shouted, "Okay! Let's break for lunch. No one's to leave the set. We'll provide you with sandwiches and coffee."

The photographer again rushed toward the stage to hook up with Sherry. Before he reached her, two hulking bruisers grabbed him roughly by the arms and growled, "Didn't Miss Silver just tell you to get lost?"

"Hey, let go of me," protested March. "I'm the one

who saved her."

"That's our job."

"Then where were you durin' the fire?"

"Never mind. Get outta here while you still got legs to walk on."

Dylan saw it was useless to argue. With a dejected frown, he stumbled away to gossip with the journalist reenactors. These men were full of wisecracks and good humor, and the time passed quickly while they waited for the direct sunlight to rise above the stage. Finally, around one o'clock, the participants took their places and got ready for Take Two.

The second take had just begun when a freak gust of wind knocked over the drummer's cymbals. The third attempt was equally futile. Sherry had just launched into her wailing vocals when her microphone went dead. They had to scratch the fourth take after a Union reenactor's musket blew up in his face. So it went all afternoon until the fuming director postponed the shoot indefinitely.

Only Dylan was still grinning as the crew filed away from the Devil's Den. Not only did he have enough photos of the shimmying Sherry to please any gossip mag on the planet, he also had the exclusive story of why her video shoot failed. He wasn't much of a writer, but he didn't need to be to report this juicy scoop.

The photographer sprinted to his car and leaped behind the wheel. Screeching out of his parking space, he almost ran over the cursing Mr. Frank. "Watch it, jerk!" the frustrated fellow howled. "I oughta have you arrested!"

"Bite me!" shouted Dylan. "Watch where you're walkin'!"

Before the director could summon security, March shifted gears and sped down Crawford Avenue well ahead of the other traffic. He passed safely through the roadblock, turned right, and blasted onto the main road. The rest of the drive was a blur. All he could think about were thousand dollar bills. And paying off his ex--for good.

Back at the motel, March set up an impromptu

darkroom in his bathroom. He threw a blanket over the window, plugged in a red lamp to see by, and mixed up chemicals in the sink. When he immersed his negatives in the solution, he got quite a surprise. Instead of Sherry Silver in her provocative bikini, Dylan had shots of a gaunt figure dressed in Confederate gray floating in front of the pop princess. He also had photos of the ghostly soldier cutting the bass amp chord with a bayonet and tipping over the drummer's cymbals with his rifle butt.

"Whoooeee!" whistled Dylan. "I can see the headlines now: 'Silver Video Ruined by Battlefield Ghost.' Man, when these pics hit the tabloids, I'm gonna be even more famous than Alexander Gardner."

With trembling hands March finished developing his film. After hanging the photos up to dry, he locked his door and went outside for a breath of air. He was quivering with excitement and drenched with sweat. To cool off, he went to the lounge to have a rum and coke. He downed the booze in one gulp and then purred to the cute waitress, "I'll have another drink, darlin', 'cause my luck's about to change. Maybe you and I can hook up later? What do ya say?"

"Sorry. The motel has a strict policy against dating customers."

"Ah, come on," wheedled March, fondling the girl's arm. "I'm gonna be rollin' in dough. Don't ya wanna help me spend some of it?"

"You'd be better off asking my grandma," replied the waitress with a stony frown. "She's about your age. Being a widow for ten years, she even might be hard up enough to go out with you."

"Ahh, forget that other drink," grunted Dylan, rising angrily from his chair. "When my pics are published, I'll have a whole limo full of chicks like you."

"Blind ones, no doubt."

"Ah, bite me!"

"Yeah, right after I get the manager."

Stifling a curse, the photographer stormed from the lounge and flew back to his room. He slammed the door and

135

locked it behind him. Flipping on the overhead light, he flung his suitcase on the bed and began packing furiously. "I better get outta here before that mouthy chick gets me in trouble," he seethed. "After I blow this joint, I'm gonna order me one of them Latin babes whose only English words are 'Yes, Daddy.'"

Dylan stuffed his clothes in his suitcase without bothering to fold them. He just thought about retrieving his precious photos when a thunderous knock echoed through the room.

"Open up, March!" commanded a gravelly voice.

"Yeah, we know you're in there!" growled another man in a deep bass vibrato.

"I'm not feeling well," squeaked Dylan. "Come back in the morning. I'm sorry what I said to the gal. Honest."

"You're gonna be a lot sicker if you don't open up!"

"Come back in the morning, I say."

The words were barely out of Dylan's mouth when his door came crashing open with the sound of splintered wood. Before the photographer could dodge into the bathroom, two thugs dressed in black military garb rushed to corral him. The burlier of the goons grabbed Dylan by the arm and twisted it violently behind him.

"Y-Y-You're not the manager," wheezed March. "Y-Y-You must be the 'associates' Bitchzilla's lawyer threatened me with."

"That's right, and we're here to collect your ex's thou," the fellow rumbled. "Where is it?"

"Well, what if I don't have it?"

"Then we're gonna hurt you real bad," growled the burly professional, twisting Dylan's arm until he squealed like a girl.

"Okay. Okay. Enough!" cried the photographer. "Show a little patience. I'll have your money in the morning. I just gotta fax a few photos I took today."

"What kind of photos?" asked the second goon suspiciously, scratching the cobra tattooed on his forearm.

"Of a ghost."

"Yeah, right!"

"A battlefield ghost. Honest!"

"You ain't ever done anything honest," snarled the bulkier thug.

"But I swear it's true.

"Then I wanna see 'em."

"Only if you. . .quit hurtin' me."

The thug released Dylan and then shadowed him into the bathroom. The photographer rubbed his arm to get the circulation flowing again before reaching to pull down one of the dry photos. "There!" he said smugly, handing the pic to the lawyer's man. "That one alone will pay the blood money I owe."

"Hey, what are you tryin' to pull?" grunted the brawny fellow, grabbing Dylan roughly by the wrist.

"Pull?"

"Yeah, this picture's blank."

"Blank? Why, that's impossible!"

"See for yerself."

Dylan stared aghast at the washed out, overexposed pic. Yanking free his wrist, he reached to pull down the rest of his photographs. A horrified expression spread across his face when he found them all ruined.

"Them photos are worthless," snarled the goon. "We'll just have to take your camera instead."

"But how will I make a living?" cried Dylan. "Isn't there some other way?"

"It's your camera or your hide," sneered the associate, slamming March against the wall until his teeth rattled.

"Okay! Okay! It's in the trunk of my rental car. H-H-Here's the key."

"You better not be lyin'. . ."

The goon stalked out the door and returned a few minutes later holding a smashed camera by its cut strap. "No wonder them pictures was no good if ya took 'em with this hunk of crap," he laughed.

"But my Nikon was in perfect working order when I

137

popped the film out of it. Did you drop it?"

"An' piss off my employer? Uh! Uh! It looks like there's only one way left to pay your debt."

"A-A-And what's that?" whimpered Dylan, noting the wicked gleam in the brute's eye.

"Ever gargled with this?" replied the professional viciously, grabbing March's bottle of developing chemicals from the bathroom sink.

"But that's poison."

"Yeah, in your hands it is," cackled the tattooed goon. "It killed all your photos deader than hell."

"But I couldn't have screwed up," bleated Dylan. "After the thousands of photos I've developed, I got the procedure down to a science. I know the time each step takes and exactly the right mix of chemicals and distilled water--"

"That's your problem right there," sneered the bigger thug, unscrewing the top of the acid bottle. "You shoulda used it full strength. Like this."

Dylan shrieked as his torturer dribbled a few drops of the solution on his bare arm. "Stop!" he cried. "Pleaseeee!"

Watching March's skin blister, the tattooed goon said, "I wonder what'd happen if we filled the sink full of this stuff and dunked in his whole hand?"

"My thoughts exactly," replied his partner. "I'll bet his ex will never be short of dough again. Let's try it an' see."

"No! No!" pleaded Dylan. "I-I-I got friends I can borrow the money from. I'll have it tonight."

"That's more like it," snickered the hulking associate. "To make doubly sure we get the entire thou, we're gonna dunk your hand anyway."

"B-B-But that's not fair."

"Like cheatin' on your alimony is."

"You get away from me, or--"

"Or you'll what? Scream?"

"Hey, that's what that Reb soldier in the parkin' lot's waitin' to hear," grunted the tattooed goon as he wrestled

Dylan toward the sink. "If he hadn't told us where you was holed up, we'd have missed out on all this fun."

"He sure was helpful, alright," grinned the burly associate. "March, when you gonna learn to keep it in your pants? It don't pay to mess with these reenactors' wives. Hey, I'll yank down the curtain so that Reb can watch us burn ya. There he is. Right behind your car."

"No! Wait!" jabbered Dylan, peeing himself. "T-T-That's the ghost I photographed."

"Tell it to the tabloids," snarled the tattooed thug, forcing March's hand into the acid. "After this, you'll never be late with another payment, will ya, pal?"

OTHER BOOKS BY
WILLIAM P. ROBERTSON

Poetry Books

Burial Grounds (Triton Press, 1977) Out of Print

Gardez Au Froid (Triton Press, 1979) Out of Print

Animal Comforts (Vega Press, 1981) Out of Print

Life After Sex Life (Four Winds Press, 1983) Out of Print

Waters Boil Bloody (Robyl Press, 1990) $5 from author

1066 (Robyl Press, 1992) Out of Print

Hearse Verse (Robyl Press, 1994) $5 from author

The Illustrated Book of Ancient, Medieval & Fantasy Battle
     Verse (Robyl Press, 1996) $10 from author

Desolate Landscapes (Robyl Press, 1997) $5 from author

Bone Marrow Drive (Chuck's Electronic Press, 1997)
     Out of Print

Ghosts of a Broken Heart (Infinity Publishing, 2005)
     $10.81 from author

Audio Books (Co-written with ShadowFox)

Gasp! The Haunted Recitations of William P. Robertson
     (Robyl Press, 1999) $10 from author

Until Death Do Impart (Robyl Press, 2002) $10 from author

Novels (Co-written with David Rimer)

Hayfoot, Strawfoot: The Bucktail Recruits
  (White Mane Publishing, 2002) $9.82 from author

The Bucktails' Shenandoah March
  (White Mane Publishing, 2002) $9.82 from author

The Bucktails' Antietam Trials

The Battling Bucktails at Fredericksburg

The Bucktails at the Devil's Den

The Bucktails' Last Call

The Bucktails: Perils on the Peninsula

ORDERING INFORMATION

William P. Robertson's books and audio books are available online at ProjectPulp.com, Barnes&Noble.com, Amazon.com, and CDBaby.com. Autographed copies can be ordered directly from the author at P.O. Box 293, Duke Center, PA 16729. See the previous three pages for prices and availability or e-mail Bill at buccobill@mail.usachoice.net. Make checks payable to William P. Robertson. Additional copies of <u>Dark Haunted Day</u> are $15.27 (postpaid).

SHORT CANDLES

Cobweb women peek from a mirror
stained with decayed teardrops.
The air is heavy with the scent
of dead lilies & a music box chimes
until its throat chokes with dust.
A ghost extinguishes short candles
before tiptoeing off to the graveyard.

CPSIA information can be obtained
at www.ICGtesting.com
Printed in the USA
BVOW06s0735291217
503870BV00004B/19/P

9 780741 432346